WARNING

This book contains adult language and violence. It may be considered offensive to some readers. This book is for sale to adults ONLY.

* * * * * * * * * * * * * * * * *

Please store your files wisely where they cannot be accessed by underage readers.

ISBN-13: 978-1773501789
ISBN-10: 177350178X

Other Books by Freddie Kim:

<u>The Time Guardian Thriller Series</u>

When the Time Guardian goes missing, it is up to Sonia to travel back to the past the rectify the future of humanity. Follow this epic tale of good versus evil in the battle to control Earth's destiny.

<u>Stinger Jacked</u>

The Free Humanity Movement (FHM) resistance hatches a plan to steal a Stinger Class assault ship from OmniClon Universal (OCU) and its alliance partner, the ka'Thar. With morale at an all-time low, Rogal and his team of misfits are sent on what could potentially be a suicide mission.

Get the latest update on new releases from the author at:

<u>https://www.freddiekim.com/newsletter/</u>

This book contains all the stories of "The Cyber Heist Files"

Book 1 – Cyber Heist

The entire financial industry of the World Government is at risk when a weaponized virus is covertly uploaded into the computer system. Faced with an imminent crisis, the government releases the whistle blower, Tyler Wilkens, in exchange for eradicating the virus that has infected their computer systems. Something malevolent is afoot and Wilkens is the best chance the government has to combat it.

Book 2 – Kill Code

When Tyler Wilkens fails to completely eradicate the virus, he is put back in prison and his competitor, another tech company, is tasked with finishing the job. As circumstances turn dire, Wilkens is released once again to do the government's bidding. But what he finds within the computer system is something ominous and unexpected. Will Wilkens be able to save the World Government from complete financial collapse?

Book 3 – Coup D'état

With the World Government ousted in the coup d'état, OmniClon Universal (OCU) attempts to take control over the world. Tasked with finding evidence to save the former government, Wilkens falls deep down the rabbit hole. With the help of Monica Franchette, Wilkens uncovers a conspiracy that leads him to multiple assassinations and the highest levels of authority. The burden of truth does not come without its risks. Will Wilkens be a marked man with a target on his back for the rest of his life?

The Cyber Heist Files

Books One to Three

By Freddie Kim

Copyright Revelry Publishing 2020

Table of Contents

Book One – Cyber Heist

Chapter One

GIORGIO KEPT his eye on the red LED numbers of the clock on the wall. It read 4:58 PM and seemed to have been stuck at that time for the past two minutes while he closed all the applications on his holo-screen. The droning sounds on the office floor had already died down as others closed their workstations and prepared to leave. He was getting impatient. Why are the last two minutes before the start of a long weekend always the longest?

The administrative offices of the World Government were going to be closed for three days. Giorgio had his entire weekend planned, but it depended on him making it on the next shuttle out. If he missed this one, then the fifteen-minute wait for the next shuttle would mean he would miss his 5:45 PM flight to Parisio. Because of the long weekend, the next available flight wouldn't arrive at the vacation city until well after midnight.

Sharla was already in Parisio, waiting in the luxury suite Giorgio had booked months before. He had planned a romantic evening, starting with dinner and then dancing. *Dessert* would surely follow later, something he was looking forward to more than an expensive dinner.

When the clock changed to 4:59 PM, he breathed a sigh of relief and pulled out his briefcase, ready to dash out of the office in less than a minute. His co-workers were already starting to move toward the exit doors. That was when his computer uttered a small 'bleep' and his holo-screen lit up from sleep mode.

Giorgio stared at the flashing icon on the computer screen. "Dammit. Wonder what that's all about?" he said mainly to himself. There was a glitch in the waste management system. These server farms, can't live with them, can't trash them. When they were first implemented way back when, they worked beautifully. Very few problems and only a small number of hiccups here and there.

Over the years, as capacity was added to handle new divisions, increased traffic, and data processing, the piecemeal build in the system architecture resulted in the use of patches to mend the seams between various systems. But the damn patches weren't meant as a long-term solution. Each one weakened the whole system.

As per protocol, Giorgio called his supervisor, Clarence, who was not going to be happy after last month's cyber fiasco. He hoped Clarence was still in his office. Otherwise, he would have to call his supervisor on the emergency line.

From past experience, Giorgio knew Clarence would never answer his emergency personal communicator outside of work and preferred to respond to voicemail at his leisure. It could mean at least a half-hour delay before Clarence would return the call. Hating himself for not ignoring the glitch and dashing out the door, Giorgio held his breath as he listened for the line to connect on the other side. One, two, three rings.

Giorgio heard the line pick up on the other side and he let out a silent breath of relief.

"What is it?" asked Clarence.

"I have a flashing icon on my screen in the waste management system," said Giorgio in a terse voice.

"What do you think it is?"

"I don't know. I haven't seen this one before. It could be the same damn crap. Should we do like before?" asked Giorgio.

"Check the Diagnostics folder. There's a new program you can initiate. It should take care of the glitch," said Clarence.

Clarence had been the system's supervisor for years, and he'd seen these types of things before. It was a pain to have to deal with these annoyances over and over again. They were always minor glitches in the system, easily taken care of by running a diagnostic program and then a simple patch program. Just one patch over another over another. It was like painting layers on a wall, it just made it easier to pick off chips.

The new program was a combination diagnostic and self-repairing program that created simple patches to fix minor glitches. It was quick and dirty, requiring little intervention from expensive programmers. The incident would automatically be logged, and somebody would collect all the occurrences of glitches and problems with the system for the master programmers to consider when building the next upgrade.

"Okay, running diagnostics now," said Giorgio, trying to keep the anger out of his tone. He had missed his shuttle, so he decided to hunker down and wait patiently for the program to run its course.

<<◇>>

The holo-screen came back to life, and the computer speaker sounded out a soft 'bleep.'

Giorgio looked over from his workstation monitor. An hour had passed, and the self-repairing diagnostic program signaled the completion of its task. The waste management system seemed to be working alright, the glitch was gone. Giorgio closed the file on the glitch and noted it in his incident report, a report that probably no one would read. Hopefully, the glitch would not occur again, but no one was holding their breath.

He looked at the wall clock. It read 6:49 PM. He had time to catch the shuttle to the aerial port. He wouldn't be getting in to Parisio until after midnight, but Sharla would be waiting up for him. He would still have time for dessert, after all, assuming she was still in the mood and not angry. And if she wasn't in the mood, he had the whole weekend to make it up to her. Fortunately for him, the romantic ambience of the scenic city would be doing the heavy lifting for him.

As he packed up his things to leave, the phone rang. Dammit, who would call this late at the start of a long weekend? Again, Giorgio felt tempted to leave, but his conscience got the better of him.

The call was coming in from the Procurement Division. Giorgio picked up the phone.

"Hey, Henry. What's up?"

"Oh good. You're still there," said Henry.

"Long story and I was just about to go. Make it fast," said Giorgio, frustration showing through in his voice. There was no way he was going to miss the next shuttle.

"Oh sorry. I'm seeing an anomaly in our system," said Henry in his usual slow drawl. "Can you take a look to see if you can fix it before we start to worry?"

Giorgio pulled up the holo-screen and swiped it over to show the Procurement system configuration. Sure enough, there was another freaking glitch in the system. One of the icons was flashing. Giorgio considered calling his supervisor again, but this was a clear case of the same situation he had just experienced.

"Henry, I've seen this before. Run a diagnostic on that system. I'll send you the file. It should be an easy fix. Nothing major to worry about."

"Thanks, Giorgio. I knew I could count on you," Henry said. "Have a good weekend."

He hung up the phone and sent the file to Henry's workstation through the government intranet. Giorgio was relieved the issue could be fixed with a simple program. After all, he had a weekend date with his girlfriend and tonight was going to be a special night for him. The thought of seeing her in the next few hours lifted his spirits and put a smile on his face. Wouldn't want to ruin it with a stupid computer system problem. Once the patch was applied, the system seemed to be back to normal.

Before Giorgio left the office once and for all, he had what he thought was a stroke of genius. He quickly composed a memo and sent it out to all division heads and supervisors with the new self-repairing diagnostic program attached. That way, if the glitch showed up again over the weekend, the various divisions could do their own repairs without having to bother him.

As he hit <Send> on his workstation, he felt a great weight lift from his shoulders. He was sure he had saved the government computer systems from a potential threat.

Giorgio was finally on his way to a well-deserved long weekend.

Chapter Two

Monica looked up from her workstation as it emitted a soft 'bleep' and her holo-screen lit up. She chuckled to herself as she read the memo from Central Systems. It was from Giorgio Karpati.

"Hey, did you see this crap?" she yelled over to the adjoining room. Through the clear acrylic window separating the two rooms, she could see the back of Craig's head and his holo-screen showing the same memo.

Craig turned his head and gave Monica a big grin. "Yep, they have no idea." Like Monica, he felt revulsion for Giorgio and his judgmental crew.

Though it was the start of Craig's weekend shift and Monica wasn't required to be there, she was content to stay. She preferred the company of machines to the people outside of work, so she spent most of her waking hours in the office. It was her prerogative. She was the boss.

With her right middle finger extended, she hit the keyboard and whispered, "Delete, delete." The memo disappeared forever from the holo-screen.

Monica Franchette, or the MF Overlord as her small team affectionately called her, looked over at the bank of L-KAT mainframe computers in the cool server room. She had been head of the division since they were first purchased. These were her babies, these massive machines. Her pride and joy.

Monica was the last of her breed, a government-employed mainframe technician. The only full-timer of her kind that the World Government had kept. That was because her division was a mistake. The original plan was to develop a mainframe backbone to govern all of the World Government's processing services and databases. But that plan had changed.

It changed when the head of the Procurement Division, Saul Pendleton, negotiated a better deal with Virtual Sentinel Technologies (VST) and awarded them the contract to supply and build an extensive network of server farms for all of the government's divisions and services.

So now the four mainframes were relegated to serve as databases for the world's registry of citizens which included information such as purchase habits of every inhabitant on Earth, DNA makeup, family tree, and other individual traits. All this information was collected through the many points of input throughout the world such as medical records, bank transactions, item purchases, teacher evaluations, classroom records, and travel history.

The L-KATs communicated with the server farms, providing real-time information when called upon.

Monica walked into the server room and ran her hand over the smooth black metal cover of one of the machines, like a loving mother caressing the tender cheek of her toddler. These old L-KAT mainframes were 34th generation ZxZ series, but they ran as smooth as the first day they were activated. Monica felt the coolness of the metal cover, the vibration of activity beneath barely perceptible to her touch.

Purring like a kitten, she said, "How are my Hell-Kats today? You don't need no stinking self-repairing diagnostic program when you have me, do you?"

Yes, she even named each one. Hell-Kat One, Two, Three, and Four.

Without even looking, Craig knew she was caressing her machines. He had witnessed it before and felt embarrassed for her. Fortunately, their division received very few visitors. When he heard her murmuring to them, he shook his head slowly from side to side and continued surfing the internet.

Chapter Three

It wasn't until the end of the following week that Clarence took the time to look at the status reports. It took him a while, but he saw a disturbing trend. "That can't be right," he said as he thumbed through the reports again to confirm his suspicions. He picked up the phone and rang Giorgio.

"Can you explain these status reports?" asked Clarence.

"After that initial glitch, boss, I started getting reports from other divisions. I sent out that self-repairing diagnostic program you gave me to everyone. Looks like it fixed the glitch so no worries," said Giorgio, who thought he had done the absolute correct thing and didn't understand what the big deal was.

"We started getting all these glitches, and you failed to let me know right away?" asked Clarence. He was annoyed with his underling, and didn't bother to hide it in his voice.

"No, I just got one call. I sent the program to everyone after that." Confused, Giorgio was hoping his supervisor would see the wisdom of his action.

"Did you know there were over two thousand occurrences? The alarm bells should have been set off after three occurrences." Clarence's voice increased in intensity and pitch, hoping the severity of the situation would sink in under the thick skull of his underling.

"Sorry, boss, I called about the first one, and when you said to use the new program, I thought it would be fine to use if the problem was the same. I'll notify you next time if it happens again," said Giorgio. Dang, it's not like he didn't follow protocol. Now his supervisor was annoyed at some small glitch that had been taken care of by a program that his office approved. Giorgio felt like he just couldn't win, and it annoyed him to no end.

Clarence hung up the phone and stared at the reports, wishing he could stop the rising fear that something wasn't quite right, and shit was going to hit the server cooling fans.

"You assured me that your company would take care of everything," said Saul.

As head of the Procurement Division, it was Saul's decision to purchase and implement the server farms. The report of the recent spate of glitches had gotten him worried. It would mean his head if they couldn't get ahead of the problem and find its source. But for now, the government systems were all performing normally.

"We're doing everything we can," said Randall. "We have our best guy on it."

Randall Easton was the Chief Client Liaison Officer for VST, and he was the one who convinced Saul that his company could deliver what the government needed. Beneath his cool, confident façade was a man close to panic mode. His heart was beating rapidly, and his hands were sweating. If he couldn't get Saul to calm down, then their little arrangement could be exposed.

"Well, your best guy isn't doing the job," said Saul. "If you guys can't solve this problem, that'll be the end of our contract with your company."

"Don't think I'm the only one who will be going down for this," said Randall aggressively. "You're the one who pressured us into lowering our prices. Plus, that extra incentive you requested won't look too good to the President, now will it?"

"Do you think you can mess with me?" said Saul vehemently.

"All I'm saying is that it'll be beneficial for us both if we work together on this, instead of against one another."

"I get it. And all I am saying is that if this happens again, I won't be able to keep Clarence from digging further into the matter." Saul threw his arms up in exasperation, feeling helpless and ineffective.

"All I can tell you is that we'll try our best. Be prepared to bail if you can. I can have a shuttle waiting for you just in case it escalates into something we're not able to stop," said Randall.

As Clarence studied the status reports, he realized there was something he had missed earlier. He slapped himself on the forehead. "Damn, why didn't I see this before?"

"Tell me," said Victor, eyebrows raised in anticipation for the answer. Victor Nugent was the head programmer for VST and was assigned to the government on high-priority cases.

"Only the systems supported by the service farms were affected by the glitch. The old mainframes held their own," said Clarence, loathing coming through in his voice.

He could just see it now. The MF Overlord gloating over the superiority of her machines. He and Monica never really got along, they had always been rivals, championing the advantages of their computer systems over each other. Up to now, Clarence was the clear winner if one were to judge based on the size and budget allocation of the government resources. But the new insight would bring that into question.

"Why do you think that is?" asked Clarence with some suspicion. Clarence raised his eyebrows, anxiously waiting for an answer from the head programmer.

"It looks like a new type of virus," said Victor. "When we track the glitch pattern, we can see it was introduced through the waste management system. Someone must have uploaded the virus to one of the stations. Our safety protocols missed it somehow. Maybe it was disguised or morphed after it entered the server bank. Let me see if I can decode it right now."

Victor fed the code fragment through his debugger and shook his head in a skeptical double-take. "This can't be right."

"What can't be right?" asked Clarence.

"This code fragment. I recognize it, but I don't know how it got here."

"Please explain." Clarence gave his eager attention to what Victor was going to say.

"Have you heard of the SNFR worm?" Victor hesitated then continued. "Otherwise known as the sniffer worm in the industry?"

Clarence shook his head, perplexed. "Never heard of it."

"The code fragment is part of the engine core of that worm. The sniffer worm was developed by one of our very own programmers, under contract to the World Government. It was meant to be used under limited conditions for the purposes of forensic auditing and for exposing activities of known terrorists and enemies of the World citizens." Victor paused, grabbed his bottle of water and took a few gulps.

"Is that a bad thing?" asked Clarence.

"No, that part is fine. It's the next part that is disconcerting. Anyway, the sniffer worm was so effective in what it did that the World Government used it to covertly sniff out every detail of every citizen who had an electronic footprint, so basically everyone."

"This code fragment was used to get this virus into places where it shouldn't go?" Shivers ran down Clarence's spine as he realized the extent of the threat.

"Exactly."

"If one your programmers developed it, then it should be easy enough to get him to look at this virus and find a way to disable it," said Clarence.

"Not so simple. Remember I said the Government used the sniffer worm covertly?"

"Yes, about that. If it was done covertly, should you be telling me all this?"

"See that's the thing. Have you ever heard of the name, Tyler Wilkens?"

"Tyler Wilkens, the traitor? Who hasn't? He divulged government secrets and was convicted for it. He deserves all the time he got," said Clarence in a disapproving tone.

"It's not that simple. He exposed the covert use of his program by the government. The government was spying on their own citizens."

Clarence shuddered with revulsion at Victor's words.

Chapter Four

Tyler Wilkens tossed the squash ball against the concrete floor. He watched it bounce up against the wall and arc back to his outstretched hand as he sat, leaning against the metal rack of his cot. One hundred. He repeated the action. One hundred and one. His goal today was to reach one thousand. He had almost reached it yesterday but meal time had broken his concentration. Today he started earlier, but he was already getting bored.

The clanking of a key at the metal door lock offered a reprieve from his regular daily routine. He wondered what that could be all about.

As two guards entered his cell, he put his arms together and extended them outward. The guards placed metal clasps around his wrists and ankles.

With one guard in front of him and the other behind, he followed the lead guard to the interrogation room.

"What's the catch? What do I get out of it?" asked Tyler. After an undetermined amount of time spent in confinement, he was astonished and couldn't believe his ears.

"We're offering you a chance to spend the rest of your sentence under house arrest, away from that concrete cage you call home," said Felix Switzer. His face remained stoic.

Tyler sensed that the Assistant Attorney General was under a lot of pressure. Why else would they send him to make a deal? Tyler's heart raced at the thought of a transfer. Then reality kicked in. He would still not be free.

"Why should I trust you? You were the one who put me here in the first place." Tyler's face furrowed into a frown. Now he was getting angry.

"If you do this, you will demonstrate repentance, and the government is prepared to show leniency. We might be able to forgive your transgressions and push for a lighter sentence," Felix relaxed his facial muscles and tried to give his most sincere look.

"No, I was betrayed by my government once. Spying on your own citizens isn't something a just government does. Passing a law to make it legal after the fact should not have been allowed. If I do this, I want a full pardon. And I have a list of conditions that need to be met." This time, Tyler spoke with more force behind the words. After all. He really had nothing to lose.

The Assistant Attorney General gave a slow, heavy sigh and stood up. "Very well, have it your way." With that, he nodded at the guard who then took Tyler by the arm and escorted him back to his cold concrete cell.

Later that night as Tyler tried to get some sleep, he heard the familiar clanking of a metal key turning in the metal door lock. He thought they might be coming to beat him severely. Maybe to death.

Two guards entered. Tyler stood up, still exhausted from his earlier ordeal. He extended his arms for the wrist restraints.

"We're not here for that," said one of the guards.

The other guard tossed a large heavy paper bag at Tyler. The prisoner had a look of confusion on his face.

The first guard looked at the second guard, and they both chuckled. Then the first guard looked at Tyler and said, "Get dressed. You got your damn pardon."

Chapter Five

Clarence and Victor sat silently by the work bench as Tyler checked the monitors and computer systems in the central control room. It didn't look like he was doing much. Clarence and Victor thought he was yanking their chain until they heard a knock at the door.

"Ah, that should be my kit," said Tyler. "Would you be so kind as to retrieve it from the courier?" He looked at both men expectantly.

"I'll get it." Victor got up and answered the door. In a moment, he was back with a heavy large duffel bag. It looked worn and smelled of moth balls.

"The government confiscated all my equipment during my internment. Fortunately, it is proprietary hardware, and no one else would have a clue about how to use it."

Tyler unzipped the bag and dug around inside. He pulled out what looked like holo-emitters and a small rectangular box. He assembled the device with confidence and speed.

"What does that thing do?" asked Clarence.

"I don't really have a name for it, but it's a 3D Emulator," answered Tyler. "I developed a program that converts the coded signals within the entire system's network into a virtual world using an enhanced 3D fractal algorithm.”

“A 3D what?” asked Clarence.

“It’s easier for me to show you rather than try to explain it,” said Tyler.

With that, he switched on the machine. A huge holo-screen lit up one side of the room. It was similar to the ones Clarence used from his workstation, except this one was much larger. Tyler rummaged through his bag again and pulled out a pair of black gloves, except that these were not ordinary gloves. These gloves had shiny black filaments embedded within the fabric, with pad-like nodes at the knuckle joints and fingertips. The gloves were activated when Tyler touched the inside of each palm with its corresponding middle finger.

With the gloves activated, Tyler moved his hands up to the large holo-screen and began manipulating the virtual environment manually. By keeping his palms open and moving them deliberately in certain directions, he navigated through the network like an expert. To Clarence, it looked like Tyler was searching for something. In the virtual environment, he approached an area that looked like a huge hole in the fabric of the network.

“This is where the breach occurred.” Tyler zoomed in on the node and revealed a serial number and the exact port where the errant code was smuggled in. “Must have been a microdrive, because the third port was the point of entry.”

A barely perceptible red crystalline trail starting from the compromised port lead to one of the waste management subsystems. Using his right hand, Tyler selected an icon from the virtual menu. A swab appeared in the holo-screen which he used to wipe the red crystalline trail. Then he deposited the swab into a virtually hidden panel to the side. A moment later, another holo-window popped up with the analysis results.

"Interesting. A weak code fragment was introduced through the breach. That's strange. How could it have propagated throughout the system?"

Clarence and Victor looked at each other, perplexed. Hell if they knew. They didn't even get as far as the weak code fragment.

"Tell me. What exactly happened after you first noticed the glitch," asked Tyler excitedly.

"As per protocol, we ran a self-repairing diagnostic program. Something new that saved a huge amount of programmer time," answered Clarence eagerly. At least he was able to answer that question.

"Thanks. That helps," said Tyler. He quickly navigated his way to the diagnostics folder and located the program that was used to diagnose and repair the glitches.

The program manifested itself as a purple fifty-eight-sided polygon or a pentacontakaioctagon. He picked it up in his virtual hands and tossed it into the analyzer. Once in the analyzer, he activated a simulation of what it would do to the inactive code fragment.

What spewed out of the simulator surprised Tyler, making him jump back a foot. His heart pounded from the shock, and he paused to catch his breath. A red blob with multiple sticky tentacles squirted out of the simulator. When it hit the network fabric, it used its tentacles to move from system to system.

"See those tentacles?" asked Tyler, addressing both Clarence and Victor. His face showed both anxiety and pride.

"Yes," answered the two spectators in unison. They were mesmerized by the show and were hard pressed to quell their enthusiasm.

"That's the SNFR component, or the sniffer part of my original program. This is ingenious," said Tyler with more admiration than disgust. "Someone was able to program a dormant virus that can bypass virtually all the safety protocols in existence for these advanced server farms. Not only that, but the diagnostics and self-repairing programs that are meant to clean up these viruses, served as a catalytic converter to transform these code fragments into something else."

"What does that mean?" asked Victor. Like everyone else, he was starting to get suspicious about what was actually going on. "The system has been cleaned, hasn't it?"

"Not from what I can see from the simulation," answered Tyler.

"If the self-repairing diagnostic program didn't clean out the virus, then where did they go? Why are the systems running normally now?" asked Clarence. Although curious, he was afraid to hear the answers.

"Those are good questions," said Tyler. "Now that we know what the virus looks like, I can build a virtual filter so that we can see what is exactly happening in the systems."

Tyler hit another menu and configured a screening filter by picking up the red blob simulation and tossing it at the virtual filter. It went splat against the filter like an insect hitting an ultraviolet bug lamp, then merged with it. Tyler affixed the filter onto a virtual beam emitter which he picked up and held in his virtual hands like a flashlight. While navigating the government's divisional computer systems, it was apparent that the red viral blobs had dispersed themselves throughout the entire system.

As he approached each blob, he pressed a red button on the beam emitter, which sent out a death ray that dried up the red blobs and turned them into virtual red dust. He did this for each system, travelling from one end to the next. As the day wore on, Tyler started looking more and more perplexed. "Hmmm."

"What is it?" asked Victor, a worried expression on his face.

"This is odd. As I go further and further along, I'm finding dying or dead viruses. Doesn't make sense. Why go through the trouble of designing something with a failure to thrive?" Tyler paused to think. "Unless…"

"That's a good question," said Clarence. "You'd think they had a target in mind."

"Wait. What did you say?" asked Tyler.

"I said that's a good question."

"No, what did you say after that?"

"I said you'd think they had a target in mind."

"Oh crap, that's it," exclaimed Tyler. "Why didn't I think of this before?"

"Think of what?" asked Clarence.

"The sniffer component," said Tyler. "It's designed to sniff out specific targets. With some minor tweaks, you can narrow down the targets even more."

"It'll take you days to narrow down and locate the specific target," said Clarence.

"Have you not met my 3D Emulator?" asked Tyler with prideful sarcasm.

Clarence remained silent, not knowing where Tyler was going with this.

Tyler pulled up the menu and zoomed out, putting the entire virtual computer system within view in the holo-screen.

All three men gasped at the same time. One section of the government computer system was completely red, covered entirely with the virus. The whole financial sector, credit records, banking processes, the foundation that drove the day to day activities of the government were in jeopardy.

Clarence backed away slowly to locate the nearest phone. "We need to call the President, now!"

-To be continued in Book 2-

27

Book Two – Kill Code

Chapter One

VICTOR NUGENT and Tyler Wilkens just stood there, astonished, while Clarence Rainer made the urgent call to the President's office.

The tech team had discovered a massive viral infestation within the World Government's financial sector computer systems. The President's office startled them even more by granting them Carte Blanche to deal with the situation. With a massive government payment due within the week, they weren't taking any chances.

"Hold on," said Wilkens. He approached one of the viral blobs. It reacted to his touch. Using his virtual hands, Wilkens picked up the quivering mass. It felt oozy in his hands, like a mass of gelatin. Swiping his hand from left to right, a virtual window popped up. He selected the magnifying glass function, and the image of the blob zoomed up on the screen. He examined it from all angles. But when he looked underneath the blob, there appeared a circular greenish glow. It was pulsating.

"Now this is interesting," said Wilkens excitedly. "I didn't expect this."

"What do you see?" asked Victor, confused.

"I configured my rendering software to pick out certain code fragments that I've identified in my programming sequences," said Wilkens. "See that pulsating green glow underneath this virus?"

Both men uttered at the same time, "Uh huh."

"Well, that's the kill code that I put in my programming," said Wilkens. "It's no secret that hackers and certain programmers will put secret backdoors or kill switches into their programs. I put in a kill-switch fragment in my coding. Only I know about it. Anyone mimicking or trying to build other viruses, even weaponized ones, will end up incorporating a kill code that renders the virus inert."

"What does that mean for us?" asked Clarence.

"Watch this," said Wilkens. He opened the virtual utility folder and pulled out an eyedropper which he placed onto the glowing pulsating greenish glow. He squeezed the bulbous part of the dropper and suctioned up some of the glowing essence. He activated another folder, pulled out a device, and inserted the dropper.

The device had a numerical keypad with selection display. Wilkens scrolled down the selection bar and highlighted Dispersion Grenade. He set the numerical counter at 1,000. Then he pressed the <RUN> button. In a matter of moments, dispersion grenades started popping out of the device.

"This is it. Everybody, pick up as many grenades as you can handle and put them into your rucksacks. I'll show you how to use them," said Wilkens.

After the device finished producing the full number of grenades and they were packed away, Wilkens and the group moved on to each virus-infected virtual corridor. He plucked a grenade out of his rucksack and pulled the pin.

"Although we're in a virtual environment, you should plug your ears and take shelter. You'll have only a few seconds to find cover once you launch," said Wilkens.

"Do as I do when we're in the vicinity of these viruses," said Wilkens. He tossed the activated grenade into the center of the infected corridor.

The team ducked around the hallway from the main corridor where the grenade was dropped. A split second later, a boom sounded, and they felt the virtual chamber shudder. Wilkens peeked around the wall to assess the damage. He signaled for the others to join him.

"The coast is clear. It's safe to come out," said Wilkens.

The group emerged back onto the corridor, but now all they saw was the red goo of the destroyed viruses throughout the corridor. They were annihilated. The gooey mass was fast turning into red dust, falling and disintegrating into nothing. The corridor was completely clear of the virus.

"Now all we have to do is proceed throughout the financial section of this computer system to clear the entire mess of viruses there. With the three of us, we should be able to rid the system of the virus in a matter of hours."

Chapter Two

"Daddy, can we go to the zoo today?" Sterling was excited to be finally spending a full day with her father.

Although Tyler Wilkens' incarceration had wreaked havoc on his marriage, his ex-wife ensured their daughter's relationship with her father was maintained. After all, he was still considered a hero to many people for his role in exposing government corruption.

The revealing of a network of spy satellites run by a secret state-sponsored agency and used to access the private lives of every citizen should have shocked the world. But instead of admitting to the embarrassment, corrupt government officials had rushed through a piece of legislation that retroactively made their questionable activities legal. Wilkens was charged and convicted of treason, earning him a permanent spot in the penal system.

But now he was free, and he needed to make it up to his daughter for all the years he had been gone.

"Yes, Pumpkin. But is that all you want? I missed your thirteenth birthday last month so you can ask for anything else. I can afford it now." Wilkens smiled at his daughter before turning his head to hide his tearing eyes.

Sterling looked at her father and cautiously asked, "Will you come to my recital? I'm playing in the school talent show."

"Nothing can keep me away. I'm so proud of you," said Wilkens, his heart filled with joy at his daughter's request.

Sterling hopped up and down with excitement, a big smile spanned from ear to ear. "Yes, I can't wait to play for you. It's a surprise." She ran up to her father and jumped into his arms.

He picked her up and gave her a big loving hug. "I wouldn't miss it for the world." But his words were uttered too soon.

As if on cue, an ominous presence seemed to hear his thoughts, and Wilkens heard a commotion at the entrance to his suite. The Assistant Attorney General, Felix Switzer, and six-suited thugs entered the room.

"Go away, guys. I'm retired now," said Wilkens with a hint of hostility. "Can't you see I'm with my daughter?" He didn't even bother to look at who was there, he was so irritated.

"Enjoy the last few minutes of your freedom, Wilkens," said Switzer with disgust. "The government doesn't like traitors who renege on their deals."

"Daddy, those men are scaring me." Sterling anxiously held on tight to her father and buried her head in his chest.

"Honey, don't let these bad men scare you. Now run along and call your mother." Wilkens released his daughter and watched her leave the room before reacting to Switzer's verbal assault. Wilkens raised his head and angrily looked at the men. "What the hell are you talking about?"

Switzer stood with arms crossed, toe tapping the ground, and cold eyes staring at Wilkens. The six thugs formed a threatening circle around Wilkens.

Chapter Three

One Day Earlier

The World Government machine had hummed along proficiently over the last three days, having recovered from part of its computer system crashing, particularly in the financial sector. The accountants and assistants made the final preparations for payments covering various contract services and debts. They also compiled the supporting documents that were due within the next two days. The schedules were set and the automatic payments ready for disbursement. No errant issues were found or anticipated.

Claire, the clerk who oversaw the entire Division of Finance, only noticed an anomaly when she did a routine audit of the payment accounts. She couldn't believe what her screen displayed, so she refreshed the system. After the refresh, the information still seemed incorrect. Perplexed, Claire initiated a full system reboot. Still nothing. Now she was worried. The system showed insufficient funds to cover outstanding payments pending over the next forty-eight hours.

As per protocol, she escalated the issue to her boss. She sent the requisite urgent email, but given the critical nature of the problem, she also sought verbal confirmation that the information was received, so she left her desk and went to the supervisor's office.

"Ms. Welles, I just sent you an email. I think you should look at it," said Claire.

Josie Welles looked up from her screen. She was just going over the divisional status reports for the week. There were many to pore over, but it was routine for her. "Can it wait? I need to finish reviewing the status reports before the manager's meeting in about an hour."

"I don't believe it can wait. I noticed a problem with the system payouts, and I think you should review it now before it gets buried," said Claire.

"You are such an alarmist," sneered Welles as she swore under her breath. This was not the first time her underling had cried wolf. There was always some disaster waiting around the corner, rain behind every cloud.

"You sent me an email, right?" asked Welles.

"Yes, I flagged it as urgent," said Claire.

"So, you did your job. Now get back to work," commanded Welles critically. She was skeptical but decided she would take a look at it after the manager's meeting.

Welles gasped in fury.

"What the hell!" she exclaimed. "Claire, get your ass in here. Right now."

Claire rushed to the door of Welles' office, terrified of her supervisor's anger. But she had given Welles fair warning. "You called?" asked Claire, trying to hide her anxiousness.

"Is this right?" asked Welles. "How could there not be funds in any of our accounts?"

"Your guess is as good as mine. I tried to warn you earlier," said Claire with more confidence, having approached the situation proactively.

Welles was definitely annoyed now. Claire's tendency to cry wolf had put her division in jeopardy. If anyone else had gone to Welles about the issue, she would have considered it immediately. But because it was Claire, Welles assumed it was an exaggerated reaction and she had taken her time to look at the issue just to punish the messenger. Now, it seemed Claire had been right, and Welles was looking bad. Claire's future in her division wasn't looking good; there would be retribution.

"We need to sort this out," said Welles. Feeling overwhelmed and fearing for her job after dropping the ball, she picked up her phone and dialed Saul's extension.

Chapter Four

Not for the first time, Wilkens found himself in the interrogation room. He was not allowed to communicate with anyone outside of the investigation, and restroom privileges were withheld. Ironically, he was allowed to drink as much coffee as he wanted. Now he really had to go.

An agent entered the room.

"I need to go to the restroom. Like right now," said Wilkens.

"In a moment. I just have a few questions for you," said the agent nonchalantly. "By the way, my name is Agent Hansen."

"I told the other guy everything I know," said Wilkens. "If you tell me what you're looking for, maybe I can help you and then go to the damn restroom."

Hansen took his time taking the seat across the table from Wilkens. He slowly removed his dark glasses and placed them in his pocket. "Tell me about this virus in the system."

"I can't tell you what I don't know. You guys won't let me anywhere near the computer system," said Wilkens with disgust.

"The deal was you were supposed to fix the system. Now we have an even bigger problem," said Hansen disapprovingly.

"If you can give me access to a terminal right now, I'll see what I can do. That is, right after I visit the little boy's room," Wilkens offered optimistically with a smirk.

"Not going to happen. Besides, I don't have authorization."

"Then let me talk to someone who does have authorization," said Wilkens. "My guess is that time is of the essence, for both of us."

"It's already been taken care of," said Hansen. "Cogent Armadillo Solutions, or CAS to you, is fixing your problem."

"You're kidding, right?" asked Wilkens in dismay. He couldn't believe his ears. "You hired a second-tier tech company to fix something that I wasn't able to fix? You must be really desperate or total idiots," said Wilkens with disdain.

"You don't fool me. We all know that CAS is your competitor. That gives them an added incentive to succeed where you failed. Because after they correct your mistake, I suspect they'll be getting many more government contracts."

"I'm not trying to fool anyone. And they're not my competitor. I'm not trying to sell the government anything. Don't you see what's happening here?" asked Wilkens.

"This is what I know, so listen up. You were given access to the government computer system. You had enough time to flush out the virus. You said the operation was successful. Three days later, the computers in the financial systems are down, and the credits have disappeared," said Hansen.

"You think I had something to do with that?" asked Wilkens. "You guys don't know what you're dealing with. You have to let me back in. I need to refine my theory on what's happening, and it's only going to get worse."

"I'll be happy to pass on what you know to CAS. They're the main team taking point now."

"I'm not giving you jack shit until I get a new deal and a restroom," said Wilkens. Sitting was becoming increasingly uncomfortable. He tried crossing his legs and then uncrossing them. Squirming around in his seat didn't help either, the frustration increasing by the minute.

"There is no new deal. All I can offer is leniency if the information you provide pays off. That is if it helps CAS solve this problem. It's only a matter time before they figure it out on their own. Then you'll be back in prison for good," said Hansen with a chuckle. He stood up and signaled for the guard to take Wilkens to the restroom before returning him to the holding cell.

Wilkens stood up for the guard. Checkmate. He felt despair, having nothing left in his game plan. What irked him, even more, was missing his daughter's upcoming recital. Would he ever be able to forgive himself? Would she? If Cogent Armadillo Solutions figured out what was happening and succeeded in solving the problem, Wilkens would lose all leverage to secure his release.

Chapter Five

The new techs rolled equipment into the central control room. The cases bore the company's CAS logo, emblazoned in bright orange and black, Cogent Armadillo Solutions. The company had agreed to a lucrative opportunity to eradicate the bug from the government computer systems once and for all. The head of the company bragged that their lead technician, Dregis, had previously worked for an elite government agency in the high-tech cyber-crimes division.

The President's office had assigned Saul Pendleton, head of the Procurement Division, a leadership role on the Task Force to eradicate the virus from the World Government computer systems. Saul knew that Dregis had worked on some of the same projects as Wilkens.

If Wilkens was unable to clear the bug from the system, Dregis would be the next best person in line to try. They kept the activity logs from the last purge when Wilkens thought he had cleaned the virus from the entire system.

Dregis studied the data and uploaded the pertinent information into the specialized equipment he had designed to deal with situations such as these. Because of the previous company's contract with the government, CAS remained in the shadows of the industry. But this new opportunity would give CAS the platform it needed to make itself indispensable to the

World Government and open the lucrative door to other potential clients.

Chapter Six

Clarence Rainer, the Systems Supervisor, observed the assembling of CAS's equipment within the central control room. As CAS neared completion of the task, Dregis, the lead technician, approached Clarence.

"Impressive looking, isn't it?" asked Dregis.

"I'll be impressed if it actually works," said Clarence. He was cautiously optimistic at this point, as Wilkens mistakenly thought he had previously debugged the system. Plus, there was the massive payment deadline looming, just a few short hours away. The impending dread wasn't helping to calm anyone's nerves.

"Although the new equipment has never been field tested on a scale as large as the government computer systems, I am confident it will do the job," said Dregis.

Clarence studied the shiny equipment in front of him. He noticed a bulky harness with multiple wires and sensor pads sprawled on one of the tables. Dregis moved past it and grabbed a sleeker, black sensory input device with one single wire cable. Attached to it was a small pad with what looked like thousands of electrodes.

"Aren't you using this wire harness thingy? What does it do exactly?" asked Clarence.

"We call it the octopus. It's the original prototype and backup of what I'm using now. The agency used it before we developed the new technology. My company redesigned it for improved efficiency."

Dregis turned around to show the back of his neck. He brushed aside his hair to reveal a white square patch that looked like a tattoo at the base of his skull. Dregis peeled the top layer of skin from the patch, to show a black square input node. The plug that Dregis had picked up from the table cleanly snapped on top of the block.

"This is the next-generation neural interface. Much more compact, easy to store, with less material to deal with. And the interface connections at the back of my neck directly communicate with the pertinent areas in the brain. You could say I can directly jack into the system," said Dregis. "We're just about ready to begin. Please take a seat and stay out of my way."

Clarence held his tongue and clenched his jaw. Dregis was clearly in the driver's seat and Clarence was just the passenger. There was nothing he could do but step away as instructed, his eyes not revealing his anger at Dregis' arrogance.

Once everything was set, Dregis fired up the system. There was no monitor screen to see what was going on, but Clarence could tell the system was activated because the equipment control panel suddenly lit up.

"Will we be able to see your progress within the system?" asked Clarence, his voice showing his concern.

"That's a negative. As it is, we had to rush aspects of the equipment to meet your deadline. There wasn't any time to add all the bells and whistles. So, no. You won't be able to see what's happening. But not to worry. I'll report fully on everything I see and do, once the job is completed," said Dregis.

Dregis activated the neural link. Clarence could tell Dregis was jacked in with his mind fully integrated with the system. Dregis' body language showed it all. His limbs tensed up and then relaxed. The chair he sat in kept his body from flopping over. The neck support kept his head upright.

Although Clarence couldn't see his face, he imagined Dregis' eyes were vacant as he focused his mind on viewing the electronic environment of the government computer system.

It was a waiting game now.

Chapter Seven

Several minutes had passed with no significant activity. The techs monitoring the equipment seemed bored and kept quiet. Every so often, they adjusted the settings, but other than that, everyone remained still.

Clarence noticed it right away. He saw a slight twitching of Dregis' left hand. And then the right hand. Then both hands twitched. Fingers undulated like little spider legs trying to run away. Finally, Dregis' body went into a full convulsion lasting for a minute or more before one of the techs screamed out.

"What's wrong with him?" shouted Clarence.

Jonas, the tech in charge of overseeing the operational equipment, looked up from his station, his eyes wide. "I don't know. I've never seen this before."

"Quick, help me release him. Is it safe to shut down the equipment and detach from the system?" asked Clarence.

"I'm not sure whether it's safer to leave him there or take him out," admitted Jonas.

"What's this red emergency button? Is it a panic switch?" asked Clarence.

Without waiting for a response, he hit the big red button. The equipment attached to Dregis' neural interface shut down immediately. The humming of the electronics wound down as the remaining power drained out of the capacitors and circuits. Dregis' body remained still, but slumped. Clarence detected a faint odor of burning flesh, probably cooked brain tissue.

Someone had called for medical assistance. A few moments later, a medic ran into the control room, detached Dregis from the equipment, and checked his vital signs.

"It's too late," said the medic. "He's dead."

Chapter Eight

Wilkens sat in the interrogation room. Déjà Vu. It seemed like the same old drill, but somehow different. Something was up. At least he now knew not to fill up his bladder during these sessions.

"What is it this time? You must have hit a snag," said Wilkens.

"I hate this more than you do. So, cut the arrogant crap," said Switzer.

"I was right, wasn't I? Did CAS screw up? I tried to warn you about them," said Wilkens.

"You can't blame us entirely. You make it extremely difficult to deal with you," said Switzer.

Wilkens sat in silence, contemplating his next move. This was new ground with potential, and he had to play his cards just right.

"The government is prepared to make you a new deal," said Switzer.

"A new deal?" asked Wilkens. He hadn't expected this. "As far as I know, you didn't honor our first deal. I did what was asked, and yet, I still find myself in this hell hole."

"Let's not open up old wounds," said Switzer. "We're running out of time."

"Any new deal we make cannot be rescinded," said Wilkens. "Every time I do work for you, I put myself at risk. I'm not willing to do that again until I know the deal is firm. Whether there's a new threat or not, I eliminate the immediate problem I am tasked with, and you honor the deal. There's no changing the agreement."

The Assistant Attorney General remained quiet for a moment. He knew it was his fault for making Wilkens a better negotiator. He nodded his head. "Agreed."

Chapter Nine

Wilkens examined the preliminary autopsy report. The MRI of Dregis' brain showed dark foci in the areas of the electrodes. Using the team and equipment from Virtual Sentinel Technologies (VST), he analyzed the data from the CAS database. With Victor in charge of the team, Wilkens knew he didn't have to worry about who was watching his back.

"Looks like his brain got fried. I could see that whatever Dregis encountered in the system created an amplified feedback loop which overwhelmed the safety protocols, sending a lethal retrograde current up along the electrodes and into his brain," said Wilkens to Clarence.

Wilkens walked over to the table with CAS equipment. He picked up the octopus and chuckled to himself.

What an ass, thought Clarence, feeling disgusted with Wilkens' attitude. A man just died trying to do the right thing.

Wilkens saw the look of disdain on Clarence's face, but he didn't care. He never got along with Dregis because of his arrogance and how he was always taking shortcuts. During their time working together at the agency, Wilkens had warned Dregis' carelessness would get someone killed. Who knew Dregis would end up responsible for his own death? Was it poetic justice?

It was apparent to Wilkens where CAS had made some ingenious strides in the technology. But they sadly lacked in other areas, mainly safety. It was like jumping out of an airplane with a paper parachute in a storm.

"I see CAS shamelessly copied technology from the agency. I recognize these as prototypes we developed back when we were under contract there."

Wilkens went back through the autopsy report and scanned the pictures. He stopped at an image of the back of Dregis' neck. The picture showed the square patch of electrodes implanted there.

"I see they developed this technology further and bypassed an entire safety layer. So, CAS was able to get the user a direct neural interface with any system they were patched into."

After a few minutes of examining the equipment, Wilkens came up with a working theory. He opened a screen to do some research.

"I need an hour to modify this equipment before I am able to proceed," said Wilkens. He looked over at Clarence who hadn't said a word the entire time.

"Let us know what you need, and I'll make sure you have it," said Clarence. He pulled out his tablet and started texting furiously.

Wilkens had his duffel bag of special equipment delivered prior to his arrival at the central control center. He rummaged through it, searching for something specific. After dumping out half of the bag's contents, Wilkens smiled broadly and pulled out a black zippered pouch. He unzipped the bag and removed a small rectangular device wrapped in cord. He unwound the cord and started soldering the connections to one of the CAS circuit boards.

"What does that do?" asked Clarence. He was further perplexed when he glanced at the screen where Wilkens was doing his research. A word kept cropping up, *Myrmecology*, whatever that was.

"This allows my equipment to talk to the CAS equipment," said Wilkens. "It will also allow external viewers to see what I do once I enter the system. If everything goes well with my upgrade, we should be ready to start in about half an hour."

Chapter Ten

"Tell me what you're doing differently from Dregis," said Clarence.

"For starters, the equipment that Dregis used was drastically deficient in safety protocols and filters. He took needless risks. Part of the software package used was ingenious, but it looks like it was hastily assembled without regard to user safety," said Wilkens. "I'm surprised the government allowed this."

Ignoring Wilkens' disillusionment and obvious attempt at posturing, Clarence continued. "Have you addressed those issues with your upgrades? I mean, you'll be safe, right?"

"Without a proper field test, it's hard to tell. But I addressed what I think are the major failings," said Wilkens. "There's no time to get a neural implant like the one Dregis had, but my modified prototype should do the trick." He held up the octopus and replaced the electrode pads extending from the wires.

A technician brought in another bundle of equipment for Wilkens. He picked up his holo-emitters and set them up on the table beside the CAS equipment. He switched on the emitters and calibrated them while adjusting the controls on the device he attached to the CAS equipment.

A moment later a holo-screen came up and showed a virtual interior of the government computer system. The resolution for these monitors was significantly higher than what Clarence and the others had experienced previously when they believed they had wiped the virus from the system.

"You still haven't told me what you think will be different from what Dregis experienced," said Clarence.

"I've studied the data, I examined Dregis' body and the CAS equipment that he used. I have no wish to meet the same fate as Dregis," said Wilkens disapprovingly. "Of course, I'll be handling things a bit differently than the amateurs. Even though I haven't tackled this specific type of problem before, I am confident. This isn't my first rodeo, you know."

Clarence noted the hubris in Wilkens' words. What was it about these tech guys and their arrogance? But right now, time was running out, and Wilkens was their best option. Clarence could afford to give him a bit of leeway in that respect, especially if Wilkens pulled it off.

Wilkens checked the monitoring equipment and readied his own station for incursion into the government computer system. A commotion broke out at the back of the central control center. It was Saul. He spoke excitedly to Clarence, then scurried over to Wilkens.

"Not so fast. We've added another condition before you can proceed," said Saul.

"Oh, really? I thought time was of the essence. You do want me to stop this virus, right?" said Wilkens. He was astonished by the government's never-ending attempt to meddle in the affairs of professionals.

"The government officials want to ensure you succeed this time. After all, you are getting a full pardon, whether you succeed or not. And for that, we want one of our own guys to assist," said Saul.

The revelation hit everybody in the room like a ton of bricks. The crew was so quiet that only the low humming of electronic equipment could be heard.

"Who would that be?" asked Wilkens with surprise.

Victor stepped forward to volunteer.

"Not Victor," said Saul dismissively.

Wilkens understood the rationale. Victor was a VST employee, not government.

Saul looked over at Clarence, who just stood there stunned. With his thumb pointed toward himself, Clarence mouthed the word, "*Me?*" He was an administrator, definitely not a tech warrior.

Wilkens looked over at Clarence and he eyed him from head to toe, sizing him up. After a momentary pause, Wilkens nodded his head and said, "Agreed."

"Don't I have a say in this?" asked Clarence.

"We don't have much time," said Saul. "You're the best qualified to represent us. You're going in. That's an order."

Clarence's shoulders slumped, and he gave a resigned shake of his head. "Fine. What do you need me to do?" He accepted his fate and prepped mentally for the task at hand.

"Relax Clarence," said Wilkens. "It's a piece of cake. I'll do the heavy lifting. You're just there as an observer. Nothing to worry about."

Wilkens walked over to a rack of surplus equipment and dug around one of the CAS equipment cases. He pulled out another octopus and modified it for the additional incursion station they had to set up. One of the other techs rolled in a chair for Clarence.

"Please have a seat," said Wilkens to Clarence as he gestured toward the chair.

Clarence took the chair as requested. "Will this hurt?" Upon seeing all attention on him as if something bad was going to happen, his heart raced, and he started to hyperventilate.

"Breathe slowly," Wilkens reassured him. "I've got something else for you."

Wilkens helped him strap in and hooked him up with the octopus.

"In order to prepare you to disassociate the physical sensations from your body and to accept the sensory impulses from within the virtual computer system, you're going to need to take this pill." Wilkens held out an off-white transparent gelatin capsule between his fingers. "It's a ketamine derivative. Once ingested, you should feel the effects of the pill within 15 minutes. It will also help you relax. Take it now. By the time we finish setting up, the effects of the pill will have kicked in."

Clarence took the pill as instructed. He followed it with a full glass of water and sat in the chair while the technicians fussed over him, placing electrodes at specific spots on his head and neck. Gradually, Clarence felt his mind disassociate from his body. It was like he was floating in the air. He knew where his arms and legs were, but somehow they seemed like separate entities from his body.

It was nearly impossible to describe. It was something one had to experience. The surroundings gradually faded from his vision and were slowly replaced with a scene within his mind of the virtual computer system. He could still hear Wilkens talking, but it didn't sound like he heard through his ears. The sound appeared to come from a farther distance.

Wilkens took only a moment to strap himself into the chair.

"Don't you have to take the same pill that Clarence took?" asked Saul, his eyebrows furrowed up with an inquisitive look.

"I've done this before, and my brain is trained to set itself in the disassociated mode at will. Therefore, the pill is no longer necessary," said Wilkens proudly. "Yes, my mind and body are conditioned to do this sort of thing. You could say I am the world's foremost expert at it."

The final preparations were made. Wilkens looked over at Clarence. Clarence was already in a world of his own, or more likely already waiting in the virtual computer world.

"Move your left pinky if you're ready to do this," said Wilkens as he continued watching Clarence.

There was a split-second delay, but Wilkens definitely detected movement of Clarence's left pinky. Wilkens nodded and activated his own neural interface.

Chapter Eleven

Wilkens and Clarence stood together in the virtual world at the main hub in awe. It appeared as a huge atrium with a domed ceiling like a wheel with hallways radiating outward in every direction from the center. Their neural interfaces added a whole new dimension to the experience as if they were in another world.

"Where to?" asked Clarence with hesitation.

Wilkens looked at his wrist out of habit, but nothing was there. "Just a minute."

He swiped his hand from left to right in front of him and activated a virtual window. From the pull-down menu, he highlighted and selected an item. Immediately, two protective suits sprouted from thin air and covered them. Built into the suit was a wrist display, but in fact, it was a Virtual Navigation System (VNS). Wilkens studied the VNS and pointed toward one of the hallways. "Follow me," he said and took off at a jog.

Clarence stumbled at first, not accustomed to his virtual legs, but he soon got the knack of it. The corridor was clear of viruses, but as they continued, the number of viruses or blobs increased in numbers. They were able to follow the path just by noting the rising number of viral blobs along the way, without consulting the VNS.

"It's just like following breadcrumbs," said Wilkens.

Clarence nodded in agreement. They stayed on the path until it became wall-to-wall viral blobs. The ground was slick, each step impeded by the blobs everywhere.

"Can we do anything about these little buggers? They're irritating," asked Clarence.

"We can, but it would be fruitless," said Wilkens. "Unless we find the source of these viruses, we'll be wasting our time just picking them off one-by-one or even if we carpet-bombed them. Remember the last time we tried it, they came back with a vengeance."

"Okay," said Clarence. He had momentarily forgotten that experience. They thought they were clear of the bug, but now it had come back in full force. He deferred the matter to the expert, Wilkens.

"Hold on," said Wilkens. He pulled up the virtual screen and punched in a few digits. Two high-powered sniper rifles and two knapsacks full of the dispersion grenades used during their last encounter materialized.

"I took the liberty of programming these beforehand. If it makes you feel better, you can start taking out some of these viral blobs. Even though it's not going to be effective in the long run, doesn't mean we can't have some fun. Besides, I've been waiting for an opportunity to play with these new rifles," said Wilkens.

Clarence shrugged and shouldered one of the knapsacks. He selected a rifle and eagerly examined it. "Thanks for appeasing my sense of security."

"My pleasure," said Wilkens with pride. He smiled and continued taking point.

They took random shots at the viral blobs without stopping. Each time they hit one, it would explode in a burst of red goo. The red goo disintegrated into a darker red dust-like substance and then dissipated into nothing.

Before they reached the epicenter of the infection, Wilkens' VNS beeped. The beeping got louder and increased in frequency as they pressed onward. Wilkens checked the VNS again. This time it was flashing and showed a focal point just ahead of them. He tapped on the flashing dot to bring up all available metrics. "This is what Dregis must have encountered."

"What do you think it is?" asked Clarence.

"Whatever it is, it looks big," said Wilkens. They cautiously approached the main node where the corridor led toward the financial systems. A low vibration and humming permeated the area.

"Do you feel that?" asked Wilkens.

"Yeah, I think we're getting close," said Clarence, trying to sound brave. The waver in his voice betrayed him.

"Not only that but notice the number of viral blobs here," said Wilkens. "We're knee-deep now." It was like wading through the muck in a swamp, each stride making a sucking sound as they lifted their legs for the next step.

Wilkens dug into his knapsack and pulled out a handful of grenades. He pulled the pins and tossed the explosive devices well ahead of them. Both men ducked down beside an embankment for shelter from the blast. The grenades went off and cut a swath of path ahead. Viral goo splattered everywhere before drying up and disappearing.

The men proceeded toward the massive object as detected on the VNS while continuing to clear the path with the grenades. Soon the humming got louder, and a constant distinct rhythm could be detected. As they rounded the corner, they looked up with widened eyes.

In unison, they cried, "Holy shit!"

Chapter Twelve

Clarence and Wilkens couldn't fathom what they were seeing. In front of them was the source of the viral blobs. It was the mother bug, and she towered way over their heads. Wilkens' rendering software depicted the mother of all viruses as a huge mechanized spider-like bug. It pulsed, releasing viral blobs from the end of its abdomen while simultaneously emitting gurgling sounds.

"Look at that mother!" yelled Wilkens.

"It looks like we found BugsE in our system," said Clarence.

"I like that. BugsE, it is. That's her name," said Wilkens.

Suddenly it all made sense to Clarence. The research window Wilkens had opened in the central control room was on Myrmecology, the study of ants. "Do you think she's like a queen ant?"

"That's my theory," answered Wilkens.

"How do we take her down?"

"Your guess is as good as mine."

The two men stood there as BugsE continued spurting out the viral blob babies at a rapid pace.

Chapter Thirteen

The men looked at each other. Wilkens signaled Clarence to follow his lead.

"Let's see what these weapons can do."

They took several grenades, pulled the pins, and tossed them beside the gigantic mother bug. They took cover as the grenades exploded. All around the bug, the red viral blobs splattered. A moment later they had disintegrated into a fine red dust and then disappeared.

BugsE remained. She was clearly agitated and uttered a horrendous screech. The sudden loss of her babies caused an increased production of the viral blobs.

"Well that didn't go as planned," said Clarence.

Wilkens' analytical mind kicked into gear. "Fascinating. There's a positive feedback loop at play. We managed to clear the current blobs, but as long as she's in the system, there will always be more produced."

"How does that information help us?" asked Clarence.

"It doesn't, really. It only reinforces what I've been saying about destroying these viral blobs before we get rid of the source. It's just a waste of time and resources."

"What do you suggest we do?" asked Clarence.

"When we lobbed the grenades at her, she did seem to be momentarily stunned. Albeit a small effect, it did affect her, nevertheless," said Wilkens. "I suggest we get a bit closer to see if we can find any vulnerable areas to exploit."

"I don't like the sounds of that. You go first," said Clarence anxiously.

With a grin and nod, Wilkens moved toward the giant bug. They approached cautiously, allowing for a large buffer zone between them and BugsE. Wilkens lead the way while Clarence remained in the rear. They made sure to stay well back in case BugsE decided to charge or do whatever bugs do.

"You flank her right, and I'll take her left," said Wilkens excitedly. "Keep the channel open on your suit-to-suit communicator. If she makes any sudden moves or does anything unpredictable, fall back to our original position. Got it?"

"Got it," said Clarence. The thought of screwing up worried him.

Wilkens proceeded onward in a huge arc in front of BugsE to avoid being grabbed by her front pincers. He maneuvered over to BugsE's left side. He then spoke into his suit-to-suit communicator.

"Clarence, can you hear me?"

"I can hear you loud and clear," said Clarence. "Go ahead."

"On my signal, lob a couple grenades at BugsE. And then start shooting her with your rifle."

"Roger that. Readying grenades." Clarence shouldered his rifle and took out a handful of grenades from his knapsack. "Give me the count."

"On the count of three," said Wilkens. "One, two, three."

On the final count, both men lobbed their grenades from each side of the beast. Grenades landed in BugsE's proximity. They exploded and destroyed the new viral blobs surrounding the mother. The force of the blast knocked the huge bug over on her side. Then each man fired their rifles into the main body of the creature.

BugsE writhed and screeched in agony, the legs on her right side bearing the brunt of her weight. Clarence, feeling more confident after watching the bug fall to her side, advanced closer. He kept firing, concentrating on BugsE's midsection.

"Watch yourself. Don't get too close," warned Wilkens.

But Clarence remained focused on his one task, no longer terrified. The adrenaline coursing through his blood gave him overwhelming courage. In a split-second, the bug righted herself.

"Look out!" screamed Wilkens.

Too late. The bug's prehensile forelegs snagged Clarence and pulled him into her waiting pincers. Surprised and without time to think, Wilkens ran up and under the beast. He fired furiously overhead into the creature's underbelly. From that vantage point, he saw a faint greenish light pulsating beneath BugsE's exterior armor. As Clarence thrashed about in fear within the creature's pincers, he kicked the armor plate and loosened it.

Wilkens realized what he was seeing. It was the creature's kill switch, except this one was protected by armor plating. Clarence had kicked it loose, but it still stayed in a protective position. The bug snapped its pincers shut, virtually cutting Clarence in half. He screamed in agony as an energy spike traversed along his neural interface and fried his brain. His body went limp.

"No!" yelled Wilkens.

In a renewed fight for survival, Wilkens tried to maneuver under the bug for a better vantage point to access the armored panel. But it was out of his reach. Then he felt his body leave the ground as BugsE grabbed him by the legs. With his upper body still free, he grabbed a grenade and pulled the pin.

But now the bug had a firm hold on him. He grasped onto the other legs so that the bug could not get his body into its pincers. He found he was right up close to the underbelly of the creature. The armor panel covering the kill switch came into view. He was close. In a swift, angry motion, Wilkens forced his hand with the grenade under the loose armor panel. He let the grenade go and anxiously pulled his hand back out. The armor plate stayed in place, trapping the grenade within.

Wilkins released his grip on BugsE's legs, allowing the creature to pull Wilkins' body up toward her pincers. He would meet the same fate as Clarence. But before the bug could chomp on him, the grenade detonated. Wilkens felt BugsE shudder with the explosion. He was thrown back several meters, the bug's disembodied prehensile appendages still grasping onto his legs.

The beast had blown up, scattering mechanized pieces and bug goo all over before disintegrating into dust and disappearing.

-To be continued in Book 3-

Book Three - Coup D'état

Chapter One

THE COCKROACH scuttled silently along the baseboard and up to the sink. It cautiously explored the toothbrush with its undulating feelers. Satisfied with its destination, it lay a sticky, viscous transparent egg-like mass within the bristles.

After finishing its task, the critter crawled back down the sink and disappeared behind the baseboard. Within the walls, hidden away from prying eyes, the cockroach convulsed and rolled on its back, legs up. A tiny plume of smoke emerged from its thorax as an enzyme pouch erupted from within. In mere moments, the cockroach body disintegrated into a desiccated exoskeleton.

The alarm went off at the usual time of 4:30 AM. Before the second alarm cycle had a chance to sound off, a hand slapped down on the bedside clock, thus ending its morning rant.

The man made a slight groan before sitting up and rubbing his face to clear his eyes. Sliding into his slippers, he stood and shuffled into the bathroom. The face looking back from the mirror showed lines of weariness, cut deep from too many difficult decisions made over the years.

Turning on the faucet and applying some toothpaste, he brushed his teeth as he had done so many mornings before. Except that this time, something was different. A sharp pain emanated from the left side of his chest. The intense pain exploded unnaturally fast. He stumbled to the floor and was dead before his head hit the porcelain rim of the toilet.

Chapter Two

Tyler Wilkens had just settled into his window seat on a full flight. He was flying on the shuttle to make it home in time to attend his daughter's recital. Since being released from prison, he was determined to become more involved in her life. And that included participating in her extracurricular activities.

His daughter, Sterling, showed exceptional promise with the viola and she was so excited when Wilkens told her on the video call that he was attending her performance. But something nagged at Wilkens from within his core. His unhindered freedom seemed too good to be true, and he tried to force it from his mind before it became a self-fulfilling prophecy.

Although he had succeeded in eradicating the virus from the World Government's computer system, the win had come too late and at great cost. The World Government missed a crucial debt payment to OmniClon Universal (OCU) and now had to face substantial penalties. The specter of Clarence's death also weighed heavily on his shoulders. Clarence Rainer, the Systems Supervisor, was an administrator, not a fighter. The government bureaucrats had insisted that Clarence accompany Wilkens on his mission despite the risks.

None of those things was Wilkens' fault, but the ominous feeling he was experiencing came to a head. Three black sedans, with lights flashing and sirens blaring, rushed onto the tarmac and blocked the plane from approaching the runway.

After what seemed like hours, four agents, dressed in black suits and sunglasses, boarded the plane. The lead agent spoke to one of the flight attendants. She pointed down the aisle, and all eyes fell on Wilkens.

Here we go again. Wilkens slumped down in his seat, trying to look small. The disappointed look on his daughter's face flashed through his mind, and it broke his heart. He hoped she would forgive him. He knew what was coming next.

Felix Switzer, the Assistant Attorney General, sat across the table from Wilkens, who had remained chained to it for the past hour. They stared at each other for some time before Switzer spoke.

"You're in deep shit."

"Don't tell me. Let me guess. You're blaming me for the failings of the World Government's effort to make the last payment," said Wilkens with a sigh and a smirk.

"You think this is a joke? You'll get life for Clarence's death. Second-degree murder. Even if it gets reduced to criminal negligence, treason will get you the chair for sure," said Switzer. "And I'll be there to flip the switch."

"I suppose it doesn't matter one bit that I risked my own life for the government. Clarence's death is on you. The risk was part of the job, and you know it." Wilkens' eyes were wide as he looked at Switzer incredulously.

Switzer stared at him for a moment and just shook his head. Then he stood up, nodding at the guard by the door.

"Lock this scum up."

Chapter Three

The World Government President, Horace Gilani, convened an emergency meeting of his cabinet. He was about to issue an executive order, something that he'd never had to do during his time in office.

All the cabinet officials appeared in the online video monitors.

"I've called this meeting today to discuss our next steps for ensuring this administration's survival. The government needs to deal with the debt payment fiasco and take care of the OCU problem once and for all," said the President.

One of the cabinet ministers, Chalmers, spoke up. "We should have never agreed to such steep concessions for accepting funds from OCU. The terms were ridiculous, and now we have a financial crisis."

"We're past the point of laying blame. You all had a hand in getting us here. I never heard a word of complaint from anyone when you benefited from the extra services and perks the credits bought. Even you, Chalmers. Griping about the situation after agreeing to the conditions in principle doesn't make you a visionary," said President Gilani. "You're as guilty as the rest of us."

"How do you suggest we handle it?" asked Sturgess, another cabinet minister.

"I propose an executive order to halt the concessions to OCU. That should buy us the time necessary to get this written into law. It shouldn't be hard to convince the Senate and the House to agree." Gilani made sure he looked each cabinet minister in the eye to ensure compliance with his wishes. "It's time to vote now. No debate or delays."

Before the votes could be tallied and announced, there was a tussle at the door. The cabinet officials reacted to similar disturbances in their respective offices. Then the video feeds cut out, and the screens went blank.

A contingent of OCU agents entered and surrounded the President.

"What's the meaning of this intrusion?" Gilani asked.

"Sir, I apologize for the interruption. I am Agent Larsen. We are placing you under arrest for the illegal act of subverting Protocol Nine." Larsen held up a tablet and replayed a recording of President Gilani proposing the executive order.

"Place your hands behind your back, please," ordered the agent.

"Do you know who you're addressing?" asked the President. "I'll have you in a cell so small, it'll be standing room only."

Agent Larsen decked the President and pinned him to the table. Another agent yanked his hands behind his back and slapped on a pair of handcuffs.

<<◇>>

Monica Franchette, the MF Overlord, sat fixated on her computer monitor, uttering a gasp every so often. News on the *coup d'état* unfolded over the day. The live streaming events were fed continuously from the many government cameras placed throughout the buildings.

The mainframe room where she holed up was insulated from the chaos. The bank of black mainframe computers hummed along quietly in the cool climate-controlled environment as if the world remained in stasis. They gave no indication of the madness surrounding them or the dire situations occurring in the other governmental departments.

From what Franchette could tell, the OCU forces concentrated their efforts on systems-related activities where the monumental viral attack was successful. It became obvious to her that the OCU overseers had set rules of engagement and were careful not to overstep their reach. Such rules would be smart, in case there was any doubt about what they were doing. If OCU had approached the take-over with uncontrolled aggression, it would have instigated a civil war.

Suddenly there was a banging at the door. Franchette looked up from her screen and glanced at her underling, Craig. He looked up at the same time, and they locked eyes in fear.

Another loud banging rattled the door. "Open up. This is Captain Orrick Smithers of the OCU

Containment Brigade. We know you're in there. I repeat, open up at once, or we're breaking in."

Franchette tilted her head toward the door, signaling Craig to open it. Craig reluctantly got up and headed for the door. He unlocked it, letting a small security force of six intimidatingly armed soldiers into the room. They entered with weapons drawn.

A voice boomed out from the rear. "Stand down!"

The armed contingent lowered their rifles. The leader walked past the tight group and paused.

"I am Captain Smithers. Who is in charge here?" He stared down the only two unarmed people in the room.

Franchette stepped forward. "I am. You have no right to be here." She held her ground nervously, wondering whether taking the confrontational response was a wise move.

Smithers looked at her and frowned. "I will decide whether I have the right to be here or not." He glanced back to one of the soldiers in the rear. "Johannson. What do you have for me?"

Private Johannson ran to the Captain, pulling out a tablet from his side pouch. "Sir, it doesn't look like this part of the system was affected by the virus."

"What are you telling me? That Protocol-9 doesn't apply here?" asked Smithers.

"No, sir. This is the only part of the system that P-9 can't touch. Only the systems that the virus affected apply to Protocol-9," said Johannson.

Smithers looked perplexed. "Hmm. That is odd. I was assured we had full rights under the terms of engagement. Why wasn't this part of the system affected?"

Franchette cleared her throat. "Don't be surprised. My department is immune to those types of viral attacks. I stake my life on it." She stepped back and swept her arm toward the bank of L-KATs, affectionately dubbed her Hell-Kats.

The Captain walked past Franchette toward the mainframes. The machines continued to hum steadily. He inspected them visually, his arms behind his back as if he was afraid the equipment would break under his touch.

He was also aware that Franchette kept her eyes on him, ready to pounce if he made so much as a threatening gesture toward the bank of servers. He intuitively knew better than to upset the protective mother-bear.

The MF Overlord waited quietly, turmoil and fear eating her insides until Smithers was satisfied.

The Captain returned to his contingent, shoulders lowered, head bowed. "Fascinating." He turned to his adjutant. "Johannson, make a note. This area is to be designated as a safe zone from here on out. No further action required."

"Are you sure, sir?" The private hesitated before making the note. This was a first for him.

"Yes, damn it. P-9 is very clear and concise. There is no grey area here," said Smithers. There was an element of irritation in his voice.

"Yes, sir." Johannson typed into his tablet, and it made a short melodic chime. "This zone has now been noted as safe and locked."

"Very good." Smithers turned toward Franchette and said, "Sorry to have disturbed you. Carry on." Then he turned toward his team and said, "Fall out. Prepare for the next sector."

The armed contingent filed out of the room, quickly and quietly. Smithers glanced back at Franchette and Craig with a sheepish smile and closed the door behind him.

Chapter Four

Wilkens was abruptly woken up from a deep sleep. It came as a surprise to him.

Not again.

One guard handed him dark overalls to change into.

Now, this is different.

They cuffed his hands and led him out, but they didn't go the regular route. They took him through passages of the prison that he had never seen before. It was obvious the route was not used very often. He could smell mold and moisture. All around him the metal bars and structures were rusted. They must have been in the basement corridor going somewhere secret, away from prying eyes.

Eventually, the two guards led him to a large delivery door in the back of the prison. They rolled up the door, and a dark transport van was waiting. It had been waiting there for a while because Wilkens could smell the buildup of fumes from the vehicle's exhaust. It was old school, using that kind of vehicle. Who used combustion engines these days? Most vehicles were electric.

After the last global war, the world switched over from combustion engines. Gasoline became very cheap, free even because no one used it anymore. Vast stores of surplus fuel sat in long forgotten tanks.

This must be something clandestine.

An old combustion engine vehicle was something that was untraceable back to its owner, the records of ownership having been purged many years ago.

While he pondered the purpose for secrecy, the side door of the transport vehicle popped open, and an armed escort came out, barking to the guards, "What are you waiting for? Load him in."

Wilkens' handcuffs were released, and he was gently escorted into the vehicle. He took a seat on one of the benches without being restrained. There were two other armed escorts within the van, keeping an eye on him.

"Where are you taking me?" asked Wilkens.

The escorts remained silent. The door to the van closed, and Wilkens felt the vehicle move. The ride was uneventful for the rest of what seemed like a long journey. He thought they were going through a lot of trouble just to get rid of him.

Almost immediately after the vehicle stopped, he heard a cacophony of footsteps right before the side door of the van slid open. A team of armed escorts motioned with raised weapons for Wilkens to get out.

One of the men outside lowered his gun, looked at Wilkens, and said, "Follow us, please." When Wilkens nodded and rose slowly, the rest of the guards lowered their guns as well. The civility of this new group of people surprised Wilkens.

He followed without question, but Wilkens was getting a bit concerned as to where they were going. Though it was still dark outside, he saw a large building that appeared abandoned. Some of the windows were shattered. The surrounding neighborhood seemed deserted. They led him inside and down to the basement of the building.

The environment was similar to the unused portion of the prison where he had just come from. He heard dripping water echoing in the distance as they walked through puddles along the cracked concrete floor. The guards may be civil, but the atmosphere was not.

They entered a large chamber and sat him on a chair in front of a typical interrogation table. This was something Wilkens was familiar with. It seemed like he was always sitting on a chair by a table. To top things off, he recognized the figure on the other side. It was Felix Switzer. Except he wasn't dressed in his usual business attire. Switzer wore a dark sweatshirt and baggy pants. He looked defeated, almost pathetic. This did not bode well, Wilkens thought.

One of the armed men placed a hot cup of black coffee on the table in front of Wilkens.

"What is this?" asked Wilkens. "Why the cloak and dagger?" He picked up the steaming coffee and took a sip. *Nirvana.* The soothing beverage took the edge off his nerves.

Switzer took a sip of coffee from his own cup before replying, "The President, or should I say, the ex-

President felt the need to make things right," said Switzer. "He apologizes for your treatment and realizes you may be the only way to find out who was behind the viral attack in the Government. He is asking for your assistance."

Wilkens shook his head. "Why should I help you? All I've gotten out of helping this government is the shaft, over and over again. Let's just say there are some serious trust issues at play here. Enough is enough, I think."

"It's not a matter of trust anymore," said Switzer. "The government you know no longer exists. And you hold the key to finding out what happened."

"Why me?" asked Wilkens. "I'm sure there are others who ex-President Gilani trusts. Even you. Aren't you his go-to golden child? Why don't you do the dirty work for him? The work I've done for the World Government has been nothing but trouble for me."

"It's against my better judgment, but odd as it may sound, he *trusts* you. The downfall of the government was a result of deep infiltration by OCU," said Switzer. "We know that you have no ties with them. And there are those who believe you have integrity."

"What would it serve now?" asked Wilkens. "The World Government is now defunct. How can I reverse that?"

"This coup is illegal," said Switzer. "It can only survive if people feel it is right. By exposing OCU's plot, President Gilani hopes that citizens will revolt and reestablish the World Government under his leadership."

"That's a pipe dream," said Wilkens. "Besides, if OCU was powerful enough to take over the government, what chance do I have? I'll be putting a target on my back."

"Yes, we understand that. That's why we're willing to compensate you with a sizable amount of ByteNuggets. As you know, that currency transcends governments and coups. Payment will be made through a third-party payment service, PayRight. I can show you proof that the funds are being held in escrow for you, to be paid out only after you complete the task."

Switzer tapped on his tablet and passed it to Wilkens. Wilkens' eyes widened as he saw the outrageously enormous amount of ByteNuggets sitting in an account, ready for transfer to him.

Switzer continued, "With those funds, you can start a new life. Change your face, move your family, go into hiding. Whatever you want. Even OCU wouldn't be able to find you. You can buy your own island and live there for the rest of your life. Just get this one little task done first."

Wilkens sat there, contemplating what he was hearing. A new lease on life just opened up for him. But at what cost? He would end up having to watch his back for the rest of his life if he took their deal. The pros and cons were bombarding his brain, and he didn't know what to do.

"I won't insult you by appealing to your sense of patriotism. We have failed you as a government. You only have two choices," said Switzer. "Either find out who was responsible for the viral attack and be well compensated or you can just walk away and live the rest of your life in obscurity. Either way, you are free now. It's your choice."

Switzer left the tablet on the table. He stood up, walked to the exit and paused. Turning back toward Wilkens, he said, "Connect the dots, expose OCU's involvement." Then he disappeared into the dark passageway, the rest of his security detail following behind.

Wilkens remained seated, staring at the tablet.

Chapter Five

Due to the dissolving of the World Government, the only evidence that it ever existed was the small, seemingly insignificant department run by the MF Overlord.

As it was, Franchette was expected to attend department head meetings and run the World Government system for OCU. Under the lease agreement, OCU would be able to access the database from the mainframes on a piecemeal basis.

The MF Overlord's responsibility was to ensure the mainframes ran smoothly during and after the transition.

Finally!

After so many years, hidden within the shadow of the server farm overlords, Franchette and her beloved bank of machines were getting the recognition she believed they deserved. Her far superior army of mainframes had repelled the viral attack that took down the World Government's entire systems network of vulnerable server farms. Her department had survived the recent government upheaval, and if she played her cards right, it would survive its new iteration, whatever that may be, going forward.

She and her team were safe, for now.

The plane took off with very little fanfare. From the tarmac, there was no indication that it contained the highest officials, including the President, of the former World Government.

President Gilani was still awaiting news of a scandal from Switzer. Little did he know, but Switzer had already lost contact with his operative, Wilkens, who was tasked to uncover the source behind the attacks on the Government's computer systems. If a conspiracy was revealed, perhaps it could be used to reverse the hold that OCU had over the World Government and forgive the missed payments.

The plane taxied to the runway and then accelerated to gain lift. Gilani held his breath for what seemed like several minutes. He knew the most likely occurrences for air accidents to happen was during take-off and landing. The plane maintained a steep ascent and made a wide sweeping course adjustment in under fifty seconds. Gilani released his breath in relief. It would be hours before the plane was scheduled to land.

He survived the first occurrence and could relax over the next few hours. There was nothing he could do in the meantime. Where they were headed, he had no idea. Communications access was limited for security reasons, and he had no idea what was and wasn't working. The only thing he could do was hope for the best, which seemed dismal at present.

Chapter Six

Wilkens pored over the software analysis data. He checked the operating system that the server farms used as the backbone of the World Government's computer systems. Doing a line-by-line comparison, he discovered an anomaly that disturbed him.

He had built a backdoor to all his software applications, as he was the original designer of the program. But the backdoor contained an additional subroutine that was beautifully crafted in that it was able to cover its tracks after making crucial alterations.

Coding had a simplistic beauty that few recognized and even fewer appreciated. It was an artform, and coding artists like Wilkens appreciated the creativity that goes into each masterpiece.

Wilkens called up the secret log for the backdoor access and discovered that there were innumerable incursions. Each incursion made minute changes in the code that wasn't significant enough to be detected. But over many years, the overall effect compromised the entire server farm. Someone was playing the long game, and they had a head start.

The end result was that the computer system became vulnerable to a sniper-wipe. All that was needed was the addition of a pro-virus to activate a cascade effect, and the whole system came crashing down like an avalanche. This was what distinguished it as a masterpiece as opposed to just another hack.

All the files were purged from the regular server farm. Wilkens performed a virtual tour of the affected system for clues. He donned the equipment that he used when he destroyed BugzE, the mother virus that had killed Clarence. But this time, he was by himself. There would be no one to pull him out in case of a problem. It wasn't the brightest of ideas, but it was all Wilkens had.

Once inside the system, Wilkens looked in every direction, in every shadow. Before, when they were hunting down BugzE, there were definite passages and hallways and a lot of infrastructure of the various system applications and subroutines.

Now, it was just an empty chamber with no discernible walls. Floating about were bits of red dust, fragments of the virus code that had since been taken apart. Other vestiges of the former program were aimlessly drifting about.

The entire system had performed an automatic reboot and reconfiguration after the debt payments were missed. Wilkens didn't have any proof, just his gut feeling, but he knew somehow that OCU was involved.

Virtual Sentient Technologies (VST) had won the lucrative contract to supply and service the World Government's computer network system, with the exception of the original mainframe system, Franchette's babies. It was his job to find the connection between VST and OCU.

Wilkens could see the new structure take shape as the computer system rebuilt itself. There was nothing more for him to find. In a few hours, the network would have completed its restructuring program.

Leaving the system, Wilkens decided to try a different tact. On the Government directory was the Records Department, where he found an area called Archives. Perhaps the old records will yield a clue, something that he desperately needed.

<<◇>>

The Archives area was located in a little-used building, separate from the main governmental offices. It was a large building, one Wilkens remembered passing almost every day, not knowing what its true function was until now.

He entered the building, which was eerily quiet. From the directory, he located the information desk. It wasn't that obvious, which was strange, given this was the place where physical records and information were stored.

Wilkens approached the desk, that was more like a window, similar to what a bank teller would be standing behind. But no one was around. On the ledge was a bell with a sign. It read – *Ring for Service*. Wilkens gave the bell a quick two-tap hit. It rang out twice. In the background, he could hear shuffling.

"Be right with you, dear."

A moment later, an older woman appeared. She was bent over and walked as if each step was torture, yet she used no cane. She looked as old as the dull and tarnished fixtures in the building.

"How may I help you?" she asked when she finally reached the window.

"I'm looking for some information," said Wilkens, suddenly feeling stupid for stating the obvious.

The woman ignored the faux pas, but her eyes held a bored look as if to say, "So what else is new?"

"I mean, I'd like to know what kind of records are stored here?" Wilkens felt a bit better with the new start.

"Oh, my. You must be new."

"I suppose you don't get very many visitors?" asked Wilkens.

"No, you're right, dear. Only historians. And only a few times a year." The woman drew forth a visitor log. "Sign here, please."

Wilkens chuckled as he grabbed a chewed-up pen from the penholder. This was so old school.

As he signed the visitor log, the woman said, "The records are hard copies. From before everything went digital."

"How far back does it go?" asked Wilkens.

"The most recent physical records are at least twenty years old now, dear."

"Nothing more recent?" asked Wilkens.

"No. Once the system went digital, everything was backed up in the electronic systems."

"Does that mean the recent virus wouldn't have affected anything here?"

"My, aren't you the little genius," said the woman.

Feeling a bit chagrined, Wilkens continued. "If the government stopped keeping hard copies of records, why is this all still here? Why are you still around?"

"Silly man. It wasn't in the budget to digitize everything all at once. The records here are kept for fifty years. We have another thirty years to go before all the records are destroyed. I'm afraid that will be after my time."

"What happens to the older records after fifty years?"

"Those records are digitized before they are destroyed."

"You're telling me that the oldest records here are fifty years old."

"Well, that was the theory. Budget cuts and staff layoffs have thrown a wrench in the works. As a cost-cutting measure, destruction of the older records was halted. In fact, we are storing records that are much older than we would normally. Who knows what you'll find down there now." The old woman let out a short cackle as if laughing at a private joke. "Was there anything in particular that you wanted to see?"

"Yes, I want to locate the earliest records available for OmniClon Universal and its registration for incorporation." Wilkens didn't feel hopeful, but he had to explore all avenues.

"Let me check. Yes, those records are in the Archives. Here is the call number for it. ZLS-149. Here is a map of where the sections are located. If you have trouble finding anything, just use the intercom system on each floor. They all reroute back to me up here."

"Thank you for your help." Wilkens went to the subfloor sections to locate the records. He was able to find the articles of incorporation for OCU. But there were no documents for VST. The corporation must have formed after the system switched over to digital.

Wilkens returned to the information desk.

"Did you find everything you needed?" asked the woman.

"No, I couldn't locate any documents regarding Virtual Sentient Technologies."

"Have you tried the mainframes?" asked the woman.

"No, why would I do that?" asked Wilkens.

"You never know, young man. The mainframes were initially used to back up all the Government records until they upgraded to that snazzy new system."

Wilkens was surprised by what he heard. It was a long shot, but he had nothing else to go on. He braced himself for the visit. The MF Overlord's reputation preceded her, and Wilkens had no interest in becoming cannon fodder.

Chapter Seven

"No fucking way are you going to touch my babies!" yelled Franchette.

"Look, you would be doing me a solid," said Wilkens. "If there's anything I can do for you in return, let me know."

Franchette paused for a moment to consider. This was Wilkens, and she had heard the stories of his exploits. He was the talk of the town, and everybody considered him a hero.

She had always wanted to dine at *Le Chateau*, having heard the filet mignon was to die for. But she was never able to get reservations. The fact she found Wilkens rather cute was an added bonus. When he offered to do anything for her, she couldn't resist.

"There is one thing you can do for me. That is if you're up to the challenge," said Franchette suggestively.

"Try me," said Wilkens.

"I'll let you peek in my mainframes in exchange for dinner at *Le Chateau*," said Franchette.

Wilkens paused. He was caught by surprise. He had always kept a respectful distance from the MF Overlord because of her reputation. She was attractive in her own way, but he never thought a guy like him would appeal to a woman like her. But this new development intrigued him. He often dined at *Le Chateau*, and never had a problem getting his favorite table.

"Hell, if you find what I'm looking for, I'll throw in a limo ride, to and from the restaurant," he said before she could change her mind.

"You let me sneak a peek under your drawers and dinner is on me," said Wilkens.

Franchette almost seemed to purr as she reached out and caressed his face. "I like how you think. Grrrr."

Although Franchette allowed Wilkens access to the mainframe, that didn't mean he was allowed to sit at the workstation of the mainframe and do whatever he wanted. He had to tell Franchette what he wanted, and she would input the search query. That didn't surprise him at all. If they ever did get to go out to dinner, he planned to order for her and let her idly watch him do it. Let's see how she liked that.

Wilkens had no high hopes of finding any helpful or revealing results. It didn't seem worth it, the price he had to pay to get at information that was potentially non-existent. Franchette worked in silence, mumbling search combination queries to herself every so often. He remained seated beside Franchette, fidgeting with his tablet for what seemed like an eternity when she finally spoke.

"There's nothing here."

Wilkens lowered his tablet and slumped in the seat. "You found nothing?"

"I've searched high and low. If there were any documents with a hint of OCU or VST in them, I would have found them. The only thing that shows up is a folder of corporate party pics." Franchette clicked on the folder and browsed through the images. "Team building shit, that sort of stuff."

Franchette continued to browse through the albums as Wilkens contemplated his next move, glancing over at the pictures every so often.

Suddenly, one of the images that flashed by caught his eye. "Wait!"

"What? What did you see?" asked Franchette as she paused her browsing.

"Go back."

She went back slowly through the photos in reverse order, one by one, stopping sporadically at what she thought was the image Wilkens wanted.

"Nope. Keep going. I'll tell you when to stop," said Wilkens in an impatient tone.

Franchette continued on, examining the photos as they lit up the screen.

"Stop," exclaimed Wilkens. His face lit up with excitement.

Franchette looked at the picture, and all she could see was a handful of young men and women in a group shot. It was an old photo, and the only person she recognized was a young Allistar Cruikshank, the CEO of OCU. "What's so special about this picture?"

"This is our smoking gun. Don't you see? It's the connection between OCU and VST." He pointed at the figure of one of the gentlemen in the photo. "That there is the CEO of VST, Charles Rendall."

Wilkens recognized many others as well. There were top OCU officials and CEOs of OCU's other known and unknown subsidiaries.

At that moment, it all became clear to Wilkens. He surmised that the only way a backdoor subroutine could have been added to affect the government's computer system on such a global level was if it was sanctioned at the top corporate level. At Charles Rendall's level.

VST ensured that the system would halt, based on the program parameters that the mother company, OCU, had decreed. Unbeknownst to the world, OCU had pulled the strings of the various smaller corporations that had government contracts in critical areas and functions. OCU made sure of that. Even the World Government security protocols were developed by an outside firm that had hidden ties with OCU.

Wilkens recognized the various figures in the image. They were all CEOs of different high-tech companies, most with no known affiliation with OCU. But this photo proved otherwise.

That was how OCU was able to keep close tabs on what the President and his cabinet were about to do with the executive order. As soon as certain keywords were uttered, it activated a recording to capture the moment for evidence.

Of course, OCU had anticipated the government's actions and had their forces ready to take action simultaneously across the globe in each minister's government office.

Wilkens knew he couldn't get close to OCU's CEO, Allistar Cruikshank, without exposing himself at great risk. His next best choice would be to confront the CEO of VST, Charles Rendall, who would know more about the possibilities for sabotage. Wilkens slapped the table, put on his coat and headed toward the door.

"Hey, wait a minute. What about dinner?" yelled Franchette, before Wilkens could make his escape.

"Oh, we're on. I've already got a wine picked out," Wilkens yelled back.

The thought of dinner with the sultry MF Overlord flashed briefly through his mind, but at that moment, he had a more pressing issue to deal with. Time to visit the VST head office.

"I'm investigating the incident of the virus that attacked the World Government computer systems, and I need to speak to Charles Rendall, your CEO," asked Wilkens.

The receptionist looked up at Wilkens as if she had seen a ghost. She stopped her typing and straightened her shirt. Clearing her throat, she said, "I'm afraid to inform you that Mr. Rendall recently passed on."

Wilkens did a double take and paused to let the information sink in. "What do you mean, he passed on? When did this happen?"

"Believe me. We're as surprised as you are."

"How did he die?"

"They found him this morning in his penthouse suite." The receptionist paused and looked around to see if anyone was listening. Then she whispered, "Rumor has it, they think it was a heart attack, but the results of the autopsy still need to be determined and announced. You didn't hear it from me."

"Thank you for your time," said Wilkens. This was a dead-end, but it seemed suspicious. He considered visiting the morgue, but knew he could just hack into the government system to find out everything he needed. Also, he didn't like the thought of examining a dead body. Better to leave that to the experts. They had stronger stomachs.

Instead, he made a detour to his warehouse to pick up some equipment before heading to Rendall's penthouse. It might still be cordoned off from visitors so he could work in peace. Wilkens wasn't sure who he could trust anymore. Well, except for maybe Franchette.

When Wilkens arrived at Rendall's penthouse, there were no barriers to entry. That meant the authorities didn't suspect any foul play, yet.

Wilkens easily jigged the lock to gain entry. Everything was clean and tidy. Just the bed was unmade.

He canvased the unit and thought to himself that there wasn't anything useful there. His tablet chimed. He had set it to let him know when an autopsy report was filed in the coroner's computer system. Perhaps it would lend a clue as to what he should be looking for.

He accessed the report and scanned it. Time of death was estimated as 4:40 AM. The deceased was discovered in the bathroom, on the floor.

If I were getting up that early, I would also be doing my daily wake-up morning routine and be in the bathroom.

Wilkens checked out the alarm clock and saw that it was set for a 4:30 AM wakeup chime.

Wilkens entered the bathroom and examined everything in great detail. A toothbrush was lying in the sink, the bubbly white residue of what would have been a mixture of saliva and toothpaste still clinging to the bristles. Rendall must have been brushing his teeth when he collapsed.

On a hunch, Wilkens pulled out a device from his backpack. He turned it on and scanned the room. He went over it once quickly and found nothing. Then he decided to do a deeper, more thorough scan by running the device closer to the floor along the baseboards.

The screen lit up on the third pass using a different setting, and an image flashed in bright red. Whatever it was, the image source was located behind the baseboard by the sink. It was buried deep within the wall.

Wilkens removed his backpack and rummaged through it, pulling out a crowbar. With it, he pried back the baseboard and shined his flashlight along the revealed crevice.

He scanned the baseboard again and studied the image. It looked like some sort of bug. From his jacket pocket, he pulled out a pair of forceps and dug around the crevice behind the baseboard.

He pulled out what seemed to be the remains of a cockroach. Except this cockroach looked manufactured. It was a good replica, but its insides were dissolved and coalesced into a minuscule dab of brownish goo.

The scanner showed that the residue contained formic acid. Wilkens pressed a button on the scanner marked <Reconstruct>. Immediately, the scanner software began to create an image based on the remains. As he suspected, the completed image was that of a cockroach.

Wilkens had read of such advanced nanotechnology, but had never heard of it being used in an assassination. There were only a few poisons that would fit the bill. He took a swab and used it to absorb the brown goo from within the bug's exoskeleton.

Just then, he heard the penthouse front door close and footsteps walking around the living room. He quickly stowed the swab in his bag and hid behind the bathroom door. Peeking around the door, he looked at the hall reflection from the bathroom mirror.

A man was searching the apartment, looking for something specific it seemed. He was armed and didn't look friendly. This was not someone Wilkens wanted to run into on the street, much less in an enclosed penthouse with limited exits. Wilkens packed up his gear and waited for an opportunity to escape undetected or at least unharmed.

As the man walked out onto the balcony, Wilkens made his move. He ran to the door, opened it and started to exit. A shot rang out, and something hit the doorjamb by his head. The doorjamb shattered, throwing shards of wood into the right side of Wilkens' face.

The pain caused his right eye to shut tight, and he stumbled sideways, hitting the doorjamb on the other side. Fortunately, it stopped him from collapsing. Blood trickled down his face from the wound. Half-blinded, he ran toward the stairwell by the elevator as two more shots whizzed by, barely missing him.

Just as he approached the door to the stairwell, the elevator dinged.

What timing!

The elevator door had opened by the time he reached it, revealing a group of rowdy convention attendees. They hastily made room for Wilkens, gasping at the sight of his bloodied face and allowing him extra standing room.

Just before the elevator doors closed, Wilkens turned around and saw the dark figure of the would-be killer disappear behind the doorway of the stairwell at the other end of the penthouse floor.

Wilkens had literally dodged those bullets.

Chapter Eight

Monica Franchette arrived at the warehouse after getting off the transit system and walking through a busy shopping complex toward the industrial district. As instructed, she ensured she wasn't followed before ducking into an alleyway. At the third building, she stopped at a faded gray metal door and rang the buzzer. She looked at the camera above the doorway. An electronic latch unlocked, and Franchette pushed the door open.

The hallway was dark, but a dim light at the end other end invited her in.

"I'm in here."

Franchette recognized Wilkens' voice and followed it to the doorway at the end of the hallway.

Wilkens was standing beside a man she didn't recognize, and they were both bent over what looked like a portable spectrometer. Wilkens inserted a sample and looked up.

"Oh, there you are. Just in time."

"Just in time for what?" asked Franchette.

"Just in time for the big reveal," answered Wilkens. There was a hint of playful mischievousness in his voice.

"What happened to your face?" Franchette had noticed the bandage on the right side of Wilkens' face as she approached.

"Oh, this." Wilkens reached up to pat the dry bandage to make sure it was still secure. "I had a run-in with a doorjamb. You should have seen the doorjamb. No biggie."

Franchette gave an obligatory chuckle and motioned nervously toward the stranger beside Wilkens. "Who's your friend?"

Wilkens noticed the worried look on her face. "Oh, yes. Sorry, should have done this sooner." He gestured toward the fellow beside him. "This here is my tech guy, Virgil. He was my secret weapon when I was battling the virus for the World Government."

Virgil gave a short wave of his hand without looking up from the workstation.

Franchette ignored the brisk acknowledgment and studied the high-tech equipment around her. "Your workshop is impressive. I let you peek at my equipment. Maybe you'll let me peek at yours?" She looked at Wilkens with innocent, wide eyes.

Wilkens smirked. "I'm already buying you dinner for the privilege. What else do you have to barter?"

Franchette thrust out her lips in a playful pout. "I have skills."

"I bet you do," said Wilkens, furrowing one brow and raising the other. "Tell you what. If you're good, I'll give you access to my hard drive."

"Geez, you two. Get a room already," said an exasperated Virgil.

The scanner beeped, diverting Wilkens' attention. Virgil looked at the spectrometer screen and typed furiously on his workstation.

"Is this what killed him?" asked Wilkens.

"I've never seen anything like this. I can't identify it" said Virgil. He manipulated the image on the screen to try to find anything familiar with the atomic configuration.

"Can I see it?" asked Franchette.

The two men stepped aside to allow Franchette access to the workstation. She typed in a few commands and pulled out a tablet from her bag.

"I'm sending the data to my tablet. I can use my VPN to access the mainframes. If they can't identify the compound, then nothing else will." Franchette opened a gateway on her tablet and typed in a query string.

A few moments later, her tablet beeped. Franchette read the result out loud, "It's a derivative of a substance known as Compound B-184."

"Compound B-184?" asked Wilkens, all of a sudden alert.

"Why? Does that mean something to you?" asked Franchette, her brows furrowed with puzzlement.

"I'm familiar with it, too," said Virgil. "Remember those stories about it being used as a household insecticide? Anyway, it was banned many years ago due to a high incidence of coronary accidents. The link would never have been discovered if it wasn't for the works of Dr. Meinschott and his longitudinal cohort study."

"Yes," said Wilkens. "And the company selling the pesticide filed for bankruptcy. AgrariTech was the name. OCU saved the company by buying it for cheap. The CEO for that company was also in the picture we found in the mainframe."

It was a light-bulb moment for all three, hitting them at the same time.

"We know that VST was behind the faulty server farm system that brought down the World Government. VST's CEO, Charles Rendall, was assassinated, his death made to look like he died of natural causes." Wilkens looked at Franchette and paused.

"We can connect the assassination of Charles Rendall to OCU with the weaponized version of Compound B-184," said Franchette. "Will that be enough?"

"It might be enough to raise serious questions and open an inquiry," said Wilkens.

"I wouldn't hold my breath," said Virgil. He increased the volume of the news flash that was playing on the media console.

...when the plane hit the side of a mountain. The rescue operation has been downgraded to recovery status. I repeat. The plane carrying the President of the former World Government and other high-level officials has crashed with no survivors. The cause is believed to be an instrument malfunction...

Wilkens couldn't believe his ears. He didn't know whether to be happy or sad. Was he home free or did he have a different target on his back? Now that he knew the truth, who would he tell it to?

As far as he knew, there was only one obligation left to fulfill.

Chapter Nine

The limousine pulled up in front of Monica Franchette's apartment building where she had stepped out only moments before. She felt uncomfortable in her high heels and low-neck black dress, attire that she was not used to wearing. Her perfume wafted gently in the light breeze of the early evening.

Very impressive. He really went all out. The door of the black limousine opened, and out stepped Wilkens.

"Well, what do you think?" Wilkens looked at her expectantly with wide puppy-dog eyes, as if asking for approval.

"I must say, I'm impressed. Well done," said Franchette. She blushed at the thought of what was to come for the rest of the evening if this was any indication of how things were going so far.

Wilkens waited by the open door for Franchette as she approached the vehicle. He held his hand out and led her inside. Like the gentleman that he was, he closed the door, went around to the other side and got in. Franchette had never been in such a fancy ride before. They both enjoyed the trip over to the restaurant, making small talk as the conversation progressed toward a more intimate one.

Dinner was at the fancy restaurant, *Le Chateau*, at the top of the SkyLine building, a place that Franchette had always wanted to go to but thought she could never afford.

"How did you manage to get reservations to this place?" asked Franchette. "I've heard it gets booked solid for months. To be honest, I never thought you'd be able to pull it off."

"Let's just say I know a guy, who knows a guy. I can't reveal all my secrets. Besides, I'm already going to let you look at my hardware," said Wilkens.

Franchette's pupils dilated as Wilkens transformed before her mind's eye into a mysterious man who had many secrets. It was something that she was not able to control, and it showed. Wilkens looked at her with penetrating eyes, as if he knew her very thoughts. It scared her while exciting her at the same time.

The waiter arrived and set up a small table complete with carving service. Franchette looked at Wilkens questioningly.

"I took the liberty of ordering for us ahead of time. This dish requires two hours of preparation. I hope you like duck," said Wilkens.

Duck! How in the world could he afford that?

Franchette blushed again. "Yes, yes. Duck is fine. This is way beyond what I expected. I've actually never had duck before," said Franchette.

"I had it one other time and loved it. It is a taste that more people should experience," said Wilkens.

The waiter expertly carved the crisp duck into thin slices. He then placed the slices onto rice wraps, garnishing them with fresh slivers of spring onion, cucumber, and a dollop of sweet bean sauce on top.

"You eat these with your hands," said Wilkens. He rolled up a wrap with his fingers and took a bite.

Observing what Wilkens did, Franchette copied his actions and took a bite of the duck wrap. "Mmmm. I've never tasted anything so exquisite."

Wilkens watched as some of the juice from the moist duck dripped from her lips.

Franchette noticed him staring at her with lusting eyes. "Your look is revealing what you're thinking. And it rhymes with duck." She put her half-eaten wrap down and licked her finger slowly.

Wilkens grinned and handed her a napkin. "Don't get too full on this. More courses to come," said Wilkens.

The rest of dinner was just as lavish, with Franchette enjoying every dish for the very first time. She never thought food could taste this good.

After their fine dining experience and two bottles of a respectable wine, Franchette was justifiably enchanted and feeling frisky. They left the restaurant where a different limo awaited them.

"I have another surprise for you," said Wilkens.

He looked at her and gave her a sly smile. As he opened the door to the limo, Franchette could see flashing lights and heard music playing inside. She took Wilkens' hand as he led her inside. In the middle of the limousine was a dance pole. Franchette, having taken lessons in the art of pole dancing, gravitated toward it immediately.

"How did you know?" she asked, as she swung around the pole with one hand. It didn't matter that she was in a dress with a low-cut chest line. Not waiting for Wilkens to answer, she grabbed the pole with both hands and started gyrating along its length. Wilkens had already gotten into the limo and sat back to watch as she gave him the show of his lifetime.

Just as the limo arrived at the hotel, Wilkens' tablet beeped. The message made his heart skip a beat. The transfer of ByteNuggets had completed automatically, and he was suddenly a very rich man. With ex-President Gilani dead, there was no one to cancel the pending credit transfer, which proceeded as if he had completed his mission.

Bureaucrats! Gotta love them.

This was the only time he had ever benefited from their mistakes, and there was no longer a World Government that could claw the payment back.

"What was the message? Why do you look like you got away with something?" asked Franchette as she settled down beside him.

"Let's just say everything I've been through up to this point has been worth it." Wilkens put his arm around Franchette's waist and pulled her in for a kiss.

<<◇>>

The Next Morning

A double knock sounded at the suite door. "Room service," came a voice from the hallway outside.

Wilkens pulled the covers back, looking over at Franchette. She was still sleeping.

"Breakfast is here. I'll get it," he said.

Wilkens rose from the bed to answer the door. The server pushed in the dining cart containing two covered platters, silverware, orange juice, and coffee. Wilkens uncovered one of the platters and inhaled deeply.

"Mmmm. Nothing like Eggs Benedict in the morning after a night of rigorous exercise."

"Will that be all, sir?" asked the server.

"Yes. Thank you very much," said Wilkens as he handed over a credit chit as a tip.

"Much obliged. You have a nice day," said the server with a grin as he looked over at the naked Franchette, who was still sleeping.

After the service attendant left, Wilkens poured a fresh cup of coffee and brought it over to Franchette. He wafted the hot cup under her nose. Franchette stirred and then opened her eyes. When she saw the cup of coffee, she cracked a small smile.

"That smells good. Did you order us breakfast?" asked Franchette, as she lifted her head to see the dining cart full of food. "You are so sweet."

Wilkens put the coffee down on the bedside table and leaned over to plant a kiss on her cheek. Franchette shifted so that her lips locked onto his. One thing led to another while their breakfasts remained on the cart, getting cold.

While the enamored couple ignored the universe, two cockroaches skittered out from beneath the dining cart onto the carpet and headed toward the bathroom.

-The End-

If you enjoyed this series, I would appreciate your leaving a review of the book. Good reviews encourage an author to write as well as help books to sell. Good reviews can be just a few short sentences describing what you liked about the book without having a spoiler. If you could spend 30 seconds writing a review, I would appreciate it: you can review this title right now at your favorite retailer.

Here is a preview of **another story** you may enjoy:

Stinger Jacked

THE ASSAULT ship sat in the makeshift bay pending a software upgrade after an emergency landing for repairs. The cold, dry wind howled relentlessly, serving as a cloak for a pending clandestine operation.

Specialist Joseph Brunner remained crouched in the shadows. The rest of the members of the six-person tactical team were hidden, awaiting the order from their leader, Garon Rogal, to board the scantily guarded vessel.

Their mission, to steal an intact Stinger Class assault ship from the ka'Thar, was crazy, to say the least. Even crazier was breaking into an OmniClon Universal (OCU) outpost to do it. The resistance knew that the OCU had state-of-the-art equipment, making the task nearly impossible. Also, they had access to advanced technology supplied by their alliance partner, the ka'Thar. Essentially, the team had volunteered for a suicide mission.

In desperation, the Free Humanity Movement (FHM), the resistance force fighting for the liberation of humanity represented as the Versapiens, had hastily sent a small team to hijack the ship. No one had ever accomplished such a feat, and nothing this risky had even been attempted. The resistance had lost entire tactical teams to less daunting missions. But the grand prize made the cost in lives worth the risk.

Brunner was not supposed to be there. He had not planned his life that way. Although he volunteered to fight for the resistance, he never wanted to be a soldier. He thought he could contribute somehow in other ways.

With a genius IQ, Brunner was more comfortable behind a desk, punching away on a keyboard, building computer models, programming, and analyzing data.

But today, the FHM did not need him behind a desk. Instead, they needed his on-the-fly expertise with uploading a virus into the target ship's system to allow the small tactical team the ability to access the core systems and steal the ship. Brunner's skills were needed for a critical role in the mission. The pressure he felt was beyond anything he had ever experienced.

Twenty-Four Hours Earlier

"Can we trust this intel?" asked Lieutenant Garon Rogal.

"It's good. I vouch for the source with my life," answered Herm Mellitz, the Intelligence Officer.

"We need you to put a team together, and do it fast," said Commander Statton. "You have a twenty-four-hour window before the ship joins the ranks of the OCU's regular fleet. There is no telling when we'll get such an opportunity again."

Rogal furrowed his brows. The intel was like a gift from heaven, and it would be a waste not to act on it. It wasn't every day a ka'Thar ship required emergency service from an OCU outpost. Especially from an easily accessible outpost with an established routine. He perceived many areas of concern. This could be their first and last opportunity to acquire an assault ship of their own. If they failed, their hand would be revealed, and the OCU would surely tighten up security measures to counter any future attempts.

"Under normal circumstances, it would take at least a month to plan and train for such a mission, and the outcome at best would be eighty percent successful," said Rogal. "But these aren't normal circumstances. We've been hit hard by the OCU, losing over fifty percent of our forces these past six months." His demeanor hardened, having warned Command against squandering resources needlessly in low-yield, high-casualty missions.

If you enjoyed this sample then look for **Stinger Jacked**.

Here is a preview of **another book** you may also enjoy:

Tomorrow's Past: The Time Guardian Thriller Series - Book 1

Year 2428 at the Free Humanity Movement (FHM) Headquarters (50 Years Post-ka'Thar World Invasion)

THE EXPLOSION resonated throughout the cavernous chamber, raining chunks of the ceiling, some large enough to kill, on the fleeing staff below. Thankfully, most of the personnel were gone, having been forewarned only moments before.

Sonia was not so lucky. A chunk of rock, deflecting from the side of the chamber in an altered trajectory, struck her squarely on the head. She collapsed on the cavern floor, unnoticed, while others rushed around in panic mode.

Nobody thought to check on Sonia.

When she came to, she realized she'd only been out for a few minutes, judging by the continued commotion. The first thing she noticed was heavy dust in her mouth and nostrils from the broken concrete surrounding her, pieces of the once protective walls and ceiling changed now into weapons. Dry particles stung her eyes causing tears to flow, blurring her vision further. She wiped her face with a chalky-covered hand, making it worse. By the time her senses had returned, Carson, the unit supervisor, had spotted her and yelled for a medic. Both he and the medic made their way to her, dodging the debris on the littered floor.

She staggered to her feet and swayed for a moment before leaning against the wall for support. Glancing around, she saw others in rougher shape than she and waved the medic away. "Please, attend to her first." She pointed to Camille, one of the maintenance crew, who was bleeding from a head wound. While the medic went to check on Camille, Carson gave Sonia a quick once over before letting her go.

Sonia probed her head with tentative fingers, confirming a massive bump, and blinking against the pain. *I've had worse. I'll live.* She pushed off from the wall with shaking arms and stumbled a few steps. Pausing for a moment to regain her composure, she walked on unsure feet toward the briefing room and her father, Commander Garon Rogal. He'd be wondering where she was, worried about her condition.

"There you are," said Commander Rogal. He looked at Sonia then glanced quickly away. She could tell he was struggling to keep an unconcerned expression on his face. Her disheveled appearance and a scrape on her forehead didn't help matters but she knew he wouldn't comment. Sonia had a tough enough time proving herself to her peers without the top commander of the Free Humanity Movement (FHM) showing favoritism, even if it meant putting her in harm's way.

"Sorry for the delay," said Sonia. "Nothing I couldn't handle. They're getting close."

"There's a bigger issue at hand," said Rogal. "We're about to begin the briefing. Please take a seat."

Sonia grabbed one of the few empty seats near the front and gingerly eased her into it. On the screen behind Rogal, a recording of the security feed showed the attack from outside. A bright flash from the display caused Sonia to squint her eyes and then the feed went dead. Big red letters flashed across the screen.

__Enemy attackers identified—OmniClon Universal Attack Forces__.

Sonia found this amusing, despite the annoying ache in her head. Of course, this was the work of the OCU. *Who else would it be?*

If you enjoyed this sample then look for **Tomorrow's Past: The Time Guardian Thriller Series - Book 1**.

Other Books by Freddie Kim

- The Time Guardian Thriller Series

- Stinger Jacked

Get the latest update on new releases from the author at:

https://www.freddiekim.com/newsletter/

About the Author - Freddie Kim

As a child, Freddie Kim would make blanket forts and refrigerator-box space ships, both essential things needed to repel against invasion from an alien race. Freddie has never really grown up from his childhood fantasies. The inspiration that he draws from the memories of his youth is captured and revealed to all in his writing.

Connect with Freddie Kim

I really appreciate you reading my book! Here are my social media coordinates:

Friend me on Facebook:
https://www.facebook.com/FreddieKimAuthor/

Follow me on Twitter:
https://twitter.com/freddiekimauth1

Check me out on Goodreads:
https://www.goodreads.com/author/show/16961603.Freddie_Kim

Subscribe to my newsletter:
https://www.freddiekim.com/newsletter/

Visit my website: https://www.freddiekim.com/